C0052 19603

D1389301

GLASGOW CITY LIBRARIES

WITHDRAWN

'I shouldn't sleep with you again.' She raked her eyes up and lingered on the open collar of his shirt for a second.

It certainly looks as though you feel that way,' he said, sarcasm colouring his tone as he looked down at her hand, still in his lap.

She snatched it back, cheeks colouring. 'I should have learnt my lesson the first time.'

'And what lesson was that?' He sipped his Scotch.

She ran her fingers up and down the stem of her martini glass. 'That multiple orgasms tend to cloud my judgement.'

Col swallowed. 'Multiple orgasms are never a bad thing.'

'No, but they do have a way of obscuring the facts.'

'The facts?'

'That you and I shouldn't have got together.' She licked her lips, that pink tongue once again darting out to betray her.

'Your lips are saying one thing, but I know your tells, Ellie.'

'You know far less than you think you do.' She leant forward, her hand at the collar of his shirt. 'But I know when to call your bluff.'

He breathed in the honeyed scent of her...it was complex and intoxicating. 'You certainly grew up.'

She threw her head back and laughed, the tinkling sound making his blood fizz.

Dear Reader

Family is something that's very dear to my heart. When I was growing up my parents instilled into me and my little sister a very strong sense of what it means to be part of a family—the give and take, the responsibility and the reward. I'll be honest: in my teenage years it drove me nuts! But I never lacked a shoulder to cry on, a hug to ease my sadness or a high-five to congratulate me on a job well done. Looking back, I wouldn't trade it for anything.

When I started writing Col and Elise's story I wondered what it would be like for two people with very difficult family lives to come together. Elise grew up in a home where her family members didn't demonstrate their love, or any type of strong emotion for that matter. Col, on the other hand, came from an abusive home where strong emotions (of the worst kind) ruled.

Writing their story was not easy, and I might have shed a few tears along the way, but I hope you love watching Elise and Col learn to trust in one another as much as I loved writing about it.

With love

Stefanie

PS I love hearing from my readers. You can get in contact with me via e-mail: stefanie@stefanie-london.com, Twitter: @Stefanie_London, or Facebook: Stefanie London Author

BREAKING
THE BRO CODE

BY
STEFANIE LONDON

GLASGOW LIFE GLASGOW LIBRARIES	
C005219603	
Bertrams	22/10/2014
F/LON	£13.50
CD	ROM

MILLS
BOON

All rights reserved including the right of reproduction in whole or in part in any form. This edition is published by arrangement with Harlequin Books S.A.

This is a work of fiction. Names, characters, places, locations and incidents are purely fictional and bear no relationship to any real life individuals, living or dead, or to any actual places, business establishments, locations, events or incidents. Any resemblance is entirely coincidental.

This book is sold subject to the condition that it shall not, by way of trade or otherwise, be lent, resold, hired out or otherwise circulated without the prior consent of the publisher in any form of binding or cover other than that in which it is published and without a similar condition including this condition being imposed on the subsequent purchaser.

® and TM are trademarks owned and used by the trademark owner and/or its licensee. Trademarks marked with ® are registered with the United Kingdom Patent Office and/or the Office for Harmonisation in the Internal Market and in other countries.

First published in Great Britain 2014
by Mills & Boon, an imprint of Harlequin (UK) Limited,
Eton House, 18-24 Paradise Road, Richmond, Surrey, TW9 1SR

© 2014 Stefanie Little

ISBN: 978-0-263-24315-4

Harlequin (UK) Limited's policy is to use papers that are natural, renewable and recyclable products and made from wood grown in sustainable forests. The logging and manufacturing processes conform to the legal environmental regulations of the country of origin.

Printed and bound in Great Britain
by CPI Antony Rowe, Chippenham, Wiltshire

Stefanie London comes from a family of women who love to read. When she was growing up her favourite activity was going shopping with her nan during school holidays, when she would sit on the floor of the bookstore with her little sister and painstakingly select the books to spend her allowance on. Thankfully, Nan was a very patient woman.

Thus it was no surprise when Stefanie ended up being the sort of student who would read her English books before the semester started. After sneaking several literature subjects into her 'very practical' business degree, she got a job in Communications. When writing emails and newsletters didn't fulfil her creative urges she turned to fiction, and was finally able to write the stories that kept her mind busy at night.

Now she lives in Melbourne, with her very own hero and enough books to sink a ship. She frequently indulges in her passions for good coffee, French perfume, high heels and zombie movies. During the day she uses lots of words like 'synergy' and 'strategy'. At night she writes sexy, contemporary romance stories and tries not to spend too much time shopping online and watching baby animal videos on YouTube.

Other Modern Tempted™ titles by Stefanie London:

ONLY THE BRAVE TRY BALLET

This and other titles by Stefanie London
are also available in eBook format
from www.millsandboon.co.uk

DEDICATION

To Mum, Dad and Sami,
for all the laughter, hugs and comfort
that filled our house growing up.
I wouldn't have made it this far without you.

CHAPTER ONE

THE NUMBERS DIDN'T make sense. Well, that wasn't entirely true—they made sense, but they didn't tell the story Elise Johnson had hoped for. They didn't tell her that she ran a successful, thriving ballet studio. They didn't tell her that she'd be able to live off anything other than baked beans and toast this week. More concerning, they didn't tell her that things were going to get better any time soon.

She rested her chin in her hand and frowned as the grid of looping cursive swam in front of her. Maybe she'd skip the baked beans and head straight for a bottle of wine instead.

'You'll go cross-eyed,' Jasmine Bell, Elise's best friend and employee, chirped as she changed out of her leg warmers. 'I always thought number crunching was best left to the professionals.'

'What are you trying to say?' She looked up from her paperwork, feigning indignity as Jasmine smirked.

'Oh, nothing…only I remember a young girl once faking a panic attack to get out of a maths exam.'

'There wasn't anything fake about it.' Elise closed the folder containing the evidence of her dire financial situation and tucked it away in a drawer. *Out of sight, out of mind.* 'That panic was *real*.'

'And the time you tried to con your maths tutor into doing your homework for you by flashing him?'

'That was less about the maths homework and more about him—he was seriously cute. Unfortunately for me a tiny bust was not enough to persuade him...' She frowned, looking down at her boyish frame. 'Not much has changed.'

'It's the curse of the ballerina.' Jasmine slipped her feet into a pair of flats and bundled her leg warmers into her workout bag. 'Anyway, that's why God invented push-up bras.'

'Amen to that.'

A flat chest was the trade-off for the sculpted legs and washboard stomachs that ballerinas were known for. Elise's years of formal training and her short-lived career with the Australian Ballet had given her just that. It was a good body, but not one designed to win men over with flashing.

'Seriously though, why don't you look into getting someone to do the bookkeeping for you?'

Elise desperately wanted to palm that job off to someone else. Jasmine was right: numbers were not her thing *at all*. Sequins and choreography and people... *those* were her things. Addition, subtraction, multiplication—not so much.

'Yeah, I should look into that,' Elise said, brushing the suggestion off. She was doing her best to hide the EJ Ballet School's financial situation; the last thing she wanted was Jasmine or any of the other teachers stressing about job security...or her.

'Do you want a hand cleaning up before I go?'

Elise shook her head. 'Go home and enjoy that man toy of yours.'

Jasmine waved as she left the studio, leaving Elise alone with her worries. She had to figure out how on earth she was going to keep the school afloat despite her dwindling savings.

The silence of the studio engulfed her. After a long day of teaching and managing the seemingly endless administration that came with running a business, exhaustion seeped into her bones. She would worry about the books tomorrow. Tonight she was going to curl up on the couch with a glass of red and a good book. Make that a glass of *cheap* red and a good book.

Elise grabbed the broom and set off to sweep the studio. She couldn't be too down on herself. It was common knowledge that small businesses often suffered in their first five years and the studio was due to turn three in a month's time. She could still turn things around.

She *had* to. Her mother had medication and treatment to be paid for, and she was the only one left to make sure it happened. She had to turn things around.

The sharp bang at the studio's entrance made Elise jump.

'Jas?' Her voice echoed off the mirror-lined walls.

When there was no response, she made her way to the waiting room. Awareness prickled along the back of her neck; her hands held the broom handle in a vice-like grip. Someone was here.

'Hello?' She tried again.

A tall figure stood by the reception desk, a man. His broad frame was encased in snug jeans and a crisp white shirt. Dark chocolate hair was close cropped, styled. She would have known that body anywhere, but it was the scent of honeyed woods and cinnamon that threw her senses into a spin and her mind into the past.

'Col?'

There were two likely outcomes from this situation, neither of them good. One, Elise would plant an open palm across his face as she'd done once before—when he told her he was leaving. Two, she would be so completely over him that his surprise visit wouldn't even have an impact on her.

Was it possible in five years that she'd forgotten all about him? The question plagued Col Hillam as he steered his borrowed car down an industrial street in Melbourne's inner north. He had to ask himself that question, because if he didn't focus on talking to Elise Johnson his mind would wander to other, darker things.

Pulling into the dance studio parking lot, he positioned himself a few spaces away from the only other car there. From the outside, the studio was nothing like what he'd imagined. No frill, no frou-frou, and definitely none of the over-the-top yet annoyingly attractive things he associated with his favourite ballerina.

Make that *ex*-ballerina…

He pushed open the car door and stepped out, leaving his blazer on the passenger seat. The sun was setting and the sky bled shades of red and burnished gold. He'd forgotten how striking Australia was in the summertime. Heat prickled the back of his neck, a droplet of sweat running over the tense muscles there. He rubbed his hand against the corded muscle, willing the tension to ease.

Gravel crunched under his shoes as he crossed the parking lot and opened the studio door with a bang. If he'd been planning on surprising Elise then he'd given himself away. No matter, subtle wasn't exactly his style.

Photos and girlie decorations in every imaginable shade of pink ran along the wall. A recent picture of Elise showed her standing with her mother and holding a huge bunch of flowers. A lump rose in his throat.

He hadn't called ahead to warn her of his visit. Hell, he hadn't even unpacked his suitcase yet. A shower at the hotel was all he allowed himself before he hit the road. Col was more nervous about her reaction to his visit than he wanted to be. He could do business with the most powerful people in the world, but the potential wrath of a tiny ballerina was enough to set him on edge.

'Col?' His name in her sweet, husky tones sent a surge of volatile heat down to his belly.

He turned, shocked at how much and yet how little she'd changed. There was not an extra ounce of fat on her small, pixie-like frame and her gaze was the same twinkling grey he dreamed about. She'd cut her hair so that it now fell to her shoulders, but the wispy gold lengths still caught the light as they always had. He was relieved to see the burning intensity of her stare hadn't diminished over the years.

'Ellie.'

'It's Elise,' she corrected him, her tone careful, guarded. 'I haven't been Ellie for a long time.'

'You'll always be Ellie to me.'

She pursed her lips. 'You can call a dog a cat, but it will always be a dog.'

'Sounds like someone's getting their daily dose of Confucius.'

Her eyes narrowed as she folded her arms across her chest. 'What brings you to Melbourne?'

Her suspicion cut him deeply; at one point they'd been as close as siblings despite the fact that he'd wanted so much more. Unfortunately five years ago that bond had been irrevocably broken. Now he was here because he'd been dragged back to bury his abusive, deadbeat father. But that was a topic of conversation best avoided.

'Business.'

'Good to see nothing has changed.' Her face softened, but her crossed arms remained a barrier between them. 'Remember that all work and no play makes Col a dull boy.'

'I don't have time to play these days.'

'But you have time to visit old acquaintances?' She leant against the pink couch that dominated the waiting room. It took all of his will power not to drink in the sight of her slender legs encased in pink ballet tights and knee-high black leg warmers. She looked like a fantasy.

'I'd like to think we were more than acquaintances, Ellie.' Friends, best friends perhaps. Lovers?

She shrugged and tucked a stray tendril of hair behind her ear, waiting for him to speak. She used her silence to force him to continue the conversation—it was a trick he'd taught her once…back when she didn't consider him a mere acquaintance.

'Actually, I'm here with a proposal.'

Her brows rose. 'Don't tell me America ran out of socialites for you to sleep with.'

'Jealous much?' He enjoyed the flare of pink across her nose and cheeks.

'Only that you're here bothering me and not them.' She tried to look bored but her muscles were tense, her body on high alert.

'It's come to my attention that your ballet studio is going through some difficult financial times.' He cleared this throat, his hands automatically tugging on the cuffs of his shirt. 'And I have a solution that I feel would be mutually beneficial.'

'Mutually beneficial?'

'Yes.' He gave a sharp nod. 'I'd like to hire you.'

She blanched. 'You want ballet lessons?'

'Hell no!' A hearty laugh started all the way down in his stomach and burst forth with a soul-relieving boom. It felt good, and God knew he needed something to laugh about at the moment.

'No need to be ashamed—male ballet dancers can still be masculine,' she said, tilting her head to one side, studying him. 'Or are you afraid you'll need to pad out your tights?'

'You know damn well I don't need any padding down there.'

Her eyes flickered over him, as though they wanted to slide down the length of him but she was forcing her attention elsewhere.

'I don't want ballet lessons.' He shook his head, wondering why on earth a grown man would want to learn ballet. 'But I do want the advice of someone who's been a performer her whole life.'

'What does that mean?'

'It's a long story but I've got something really important coming up and I need your expertise.' He turned a charming grin on her, hoping to hell it had the right effect. Back in the day his smile had won her over on more than one occasion. 'In return, I'll make all your financial woes go away.'

She pushed up from the couch and strode towards

him, closing the gap between them. Charged and dangerous. Though he had a head and a half on her she held herself with the grace of a queen. She approached him, lips ready for battle, hands balled into fists by her sides.

Had he really breezed in here, after five years of silence, wanting her help and offering to be some kind of knight in shining armour? Impossible. No one was *that* cocky. Perhaps all those winters in New York had frozen his brain cells beyond repair. Still, Elise couldn't take her eyes off him...she never could. Col Hillam was like a drug; a very fun, stupid, dangerous drug.

He'd filled out since the last time she saw him when he'd still be wearing his lanky frame like an awkward uniform. Now broad shoulders stretched out beneath the white cotton of his shirt creating a neat V to the waist of his jeans. A dark smattering of hair peeked at her when he played with the cuffs of his shirt, rolling them up his muscled forearms. She stopped herself from lingering there for too long.

He was far from the quiet young man she remembered. Despite his flippant tone, the hard set of his sculpted lips and wary blue gaze spelled trouble. He was here with a goal in mind, and she'd be hard pressed to get around him.

'Why should I help you?'

'Because you've got a kind heart and a strong sense of charity?' There was that grin again. Cocky—clearly becoming CEO had helped him grow accustomed to getting his own way.

'Why me?' she asked.

'Because you're the only one who knows me well

enough.' He raked a hand through his dark hair, fingers thrusting through the strands in a single, swift gesture.

Each movement radiated sexual energy and masculinity. It was no wonder the single shot of him in an intimate clinch with a certain technology heiress had been flashed all over the media…not that she'd been keeping tabs.

'I'm worried for you, if that's true.' She couldn't help it—some little part of her wanted to hurt him. To pay him back for those years she spent dealing with her problems confused and alone.

Her life had fallen apart when he left as if his departure had caused an irreversible ripple of tragic events. Sure, he might not have had direct influence but it had all started with him. It had been easy to blame him when he was on the other side of the world, but now he was mere inches from her and she was struggling to stay in control.

'Ouch.' A scowl flickered across his face, but he wouldn't be so easy to tear down. 'The lady has a sharp tongue.'

'The lady also has a good bullshit detector.' She tilted her head up at him and narrowed her eyes. 'There's something you're not telling me.'

She sucked in a breath. Verbal sparring was like foreplay for the mind as far as Col was concerned. He didn't need to touch her; he only needed to pour his words over her like warm honey. She squared her shoulders. She'd promised herself she would never forget how he left her, and that meant keeping her distance. She couldn't give up that painful memory because it was what she used to shield herself against future hurt.

'Have a drink with me tomorrow, we can sort out the business side of things and I'll fill you in on the details.'

Going for a drink with Col was a bad idea. She was mouthy at the best of times, let alone when there were cocktails involved. That was *exactly* how they ended up in bed together the first time.

'No.'

'That's one thing I admire about you, Elise.' He reached out and touched her hair, smoothing the strands into place with his fingertips. 'You're so decisive.'

'I don't need your admiration.' Her cheeks flamed. How was it that he could make a supposed compliment sound so derisive? 'But you're spot on, Col, and it's with that personality trait that I can comfortably tell you to shove your proposal.'

'You don't even know what the proposal is.' The corner of his mouth twitched.

'Read my lips, Col.' She was close enough to melt against him, and she had to fight the urge with every ounce of will power she possessed. 'Shove it.'

'Anywhere in particular?' he drawled. The man was not going to back down, but she'd be damned if she'd let him pay her for anything. She might need the money, but she needed her dignity more.

'Wherever it will fit.'

'I'm not going to take no for an answer.' His large hands ran up her arms to rest on her shoulders.

A frisson of excitement shot through her as his fingertips touched her bare skin, but she shook his hands off, swatting at him with force. 'Good, because I'm not going to answer you again.'

'You know I can be very dogged when I want to be.'

One didn't become a CEO before they were thirty

without a kind of obsessive persistence. He'd wanted her for years when they were younger and she'd dangled herself like a gleaming carrot in front of him. She'd only ever given in once…and it had been enough to unsettle the entire course of her life. Yes, it sounded a touch dramatic but the day he left, every semblance of normality she had ever known had fractured and splintered until there was nothing left. Part of her wanted someone to blame, and he was the only viable candidate.

'Col, it takes a little more than repetition to get to me.' She reached for her bag and slung it over her shoulder.

'You don't want to encourage me, Elise.'

Hearing her full name erupt like a growl from the back of his throat sent her senses into a frenzy. She was drawn to the guttural masculinity that simmered close to the surface whenever he chased something he wanted. It was the one crack in his public façade and she found it sexier than anything else on earth.

'I wasn't encouraging you.'

He opened his mouth and then thought better of responding. Holding his arm out for her, he waited patiently while she took longer than she needed to walk past without touching him.

'We should continue this conversation over drinks.'

He stood close behind her while she set the alarm code for the studio. Elise bristled at his proximity, her body primed for his touch and yet retreating at the same time. Warning bells rang a crazy, maddening cacophony in her head while she chanted to herself: *don't give in, don't give in.*

'There isn't a conversation to continue, Col.'

'So turn up, I'll buy you a few drinks and you can

think about where else I can shove my proposal.' He followed her out of the studio into the balmy summer air.

Temptation curled in her belly like a snake preparing to strike. Her otherwise enviable discipline had never extended to Col. Somehow he made her forget everything she needed to do, every obligation she had, every belief she clung to.

'I'll see you tomorrow.' He brushed his thumb across her cheek so gently she might have imagined it.

He was gone before she could think to protest, leaving her to fume that he'd got one over on her. Her fists clenched again, and she took a moment to steady herself before walking to her car. He had some nerve, coming back and turning up here as if his absence hadn't left a giant, gaping hole in her life.

Feeling her phone vibrate in her bag, Elise dug through the mess of papers and beauty products to find the buzzing device. 'Hello?'

'Elise Johnson?' The male voice was unfamiliar. 'I'm calling from Victoria Bank. Do you have a moment to talk?'

CHAPTER TWO

AROUND THEM THE café bustled as though the world wasn't crashing down. People laughed, sunshine streamed in through the floor-to-ceiling windows and the cheerful sound of cups clinking against saucers scratched at Elise's nerves. Perhaps a third coffee wasn't a wise choice for someone who was already more hyper than a puppy on speed. Still, overindulging in coffee was a little better than face-planting into a tub of peanut butter and chocolate-fudge ice cream, which was *exactly* what she wanted to do.

The bank manager who called her last night had very politely informed her that she was at risk of defaulting on her loan for the EJ Ballet School studio. He'd asked her to come in and talk to one of the staff at the bank and explore what options were available, but Elise knew that without somehow increasing the money they were making the studio would be a goner. Then how would she support her mother?

The last twenty-four hours had been a mind-bender. Elise had flipped from telling herself it would all be okay to preparing herself for the worst, and with a night of terrible sleep behind her she felt frayed at the edges. Between her encounter with Col and the call from the bank, she'd barely eaten from the growing discomfort of nerves bundling tightly within her.

'Ellie?' Jasmine waved a hand in front of her face, her dark eyes narrowed. 'You still with us?'

'Col came to visit me yesterday.' She hadn't been planning on telling her friends—or anyone else for that matter—about Col's visit but the words slipped out before she could stop them.

'Wow.' Missy, her other best friend slash employee, watched her with eyes wide as dinner plates. 'That's a surprise.'

'I know.'

Missy fiddled with her coffee cup. 'It's been a while, hasn't it?'

'Five years.' She nodded. There hadn't been a word from Col in half a decade…not a peep since the night he left. 'He wants to hire me…well, kind of.'

'What on earth for?' Jasmine asked, incredulous.

'He wants to hire me to do something performance related, but he didn't tell me what it was exactly.' It sounded more ridiculous when spoken aloud than it did in her head…if that was possible. 'He offered to pay me.'

'What kind of performance?' Missy leant in, her turquoise eyes alight with curiosity. Jasmine elbowed her in the ribs, glaring.

'Like I said, I don't know.'

Jasmine shook her head. 'That sounds sus…you're not thinking about it, are you?'

Elise rolled her eyes; her friend was ever the protective mother hen. 'I *wasn't* thinking about it.'

'But…?'

'Maybe now I am.' She sighed. 'I don't know.'

'It's not a good idea,' Jasmine said and Missy rolled her eyes.

'I know that.'

'Well?'

'Well…' She paused, letting out a long sigh. 'The studio's going through a rough patch.'

Missy's aquamarine eyes widened. 'You should have said something!'

'It's not a big deal, Miss.'

'It is if you're thinking of letting Col hire you,' Jasmine replied.

'This is my family we're talking about…my life.' How else would she support her drinking, gambling, all-kinds-of-screwed-up mother?

'You deserve better.' Jasmine shook her head, letting out a frustrated huff. 'We'll find a way to get the money for the studio. We can fundraise, run a charity drive…'

Missy nodded her head in vigorous agreement. 'Anything you need.'

'It's a little worse than what a charity drive can help with.' That was it; the stone-cold truth was out there. 'Promise me you won't tell the other teachers about this.'

The girls nodded and answered without hesitating, 'We promise.'

Elise looked at her watch. She had precisely three hours in which to forget her dignity and plan how she was going to tell Col she was considering his offer… without even knowing what it was. How desperate was that? Her cheeks flamed at the thought; there was no way she should be doing this.

And yet he'd managed to make her the vulnerable party. Clearly his lure was as strong as it had ever been.

Closing her eyes, Elise forced the thought from her mind. She was doing this for the money and the money *only*. The fact that she'd wanted Col since she was old enough to understand the concept of desire was totally beside the point.

Ugh, why did she have to think about that? An uncomfortable sensation surged between her legs and Elise shifted in the hard café chair. She would not think about sleeping with Col, she would not think about sleeping with Col, she would not—

'I don't even want to know what you're thinking about.' Jasmine sighed.

'I do,' Missy chimed in with a wink.

'I'm not thinking about him.' *I'm not, I'm not.*

'Like I said, don't want to know.' Jasmine shook her head. 'I still can't believe you didn't tell us about the studio. How did it happen?'

'I wish there was an easy answer to that.'

'It's pretty black and white when it comes to finances, Ellie. What's going on that you're not telling us?'

How could she tell her best friends that her mother had gambled away their savings on a horse race? Well, on several horse races and one greyhound race if she'd got her facts right, but it was all the same in the end. No money to pay the loan on the studio. A decline in the economy meant they'd lost a chunk of their student body when their parents could no longer afford added extras like ballet tuition. Then there were the ongoing costs for her mother's medication, the fact that she hadn't been able to go back to work…

'Let's just say it was a perfect storm.' Elise sighed.

'You know I hate it when you shut me out.' Jasmine pushed back on her chair and picked up her bag.

'Lucky for me you two put up with all my crap.'

The girls filed out of the café and into the summer air. A cool breeze danced across Elise's bare arms and caused the hairs to rise. She had a very bad feeling about her meeting with Col...a very bad feeling.

By the time Col left his last meeting for the day he was drained, in desperate need of a stress-relieving work-out...and he was late.

He'd known this trip wouldn't be an easy one. He wasn't even sure why his father had him listed as the executor of his will. It wasn't as if he'd had anything to do with the man for the last decade of his life. Now he had to spend his precious time—time he should be using to prepare for a huge opportunity for his com-pany—digging around a house he never wanted to visit, looking for paperwork so he could settle up an estate that was worth nothing...probably less than nothing by the time he subtracted the lawyer's fees.

'Dammit.'

He jogged to the rental car from the shiny office building, pulling his tie loose with one hand and dial-ling Elise's number on his mobile with the other. She hadn't exactly given him her number but Col's assistant was a skilful detective, and shortly after he'd requested Elise's number it had appeared in his inbox.

The phone rang once, twice, three times—'Hello?'

Her husky little voice was enough to light a fire in his blood and tighten the front of his trousers. He was looking forward to seeing her far more than was healthy.

'It's Col.'

'How did you get this nu—?'

'Never mind that. I'm running late.' He unlocked the car and slid into the leather seat. The car was stuffy from sitting in the sun and the leather warmed his skin through the thin cotton of his trousers.

'Shocker.'

'Let's catch up near the hotel. That way I can duck back and have a quick shower before we meet.'

'I don't believe I actually agreed to meet you.'

'Tell me you're not already dressed up and waiting for me.' Silence on the other end of the line confirmed he was right. 'I'll see you there.'

'You do realise that sounds suspicious as all hell.'

'It's not a ploy, Ellie. I really want a shower…though you're free to join me if you feel like saving on your water bill.'

'Where are we meeting?' She wasn't going to bite… unfortunately.

'That little bar under the bridge on Southbank. It's the one—'

'I know which one it is.'

'See you there in an hour?'

Click. He'd take that as a confirmation.

An hour and a half later Col arrived at their meeting place and looked around for Elise. The open-air bar was attached to the bridge that ran over the Yarra River. Only in Melbourne would you find a bar suspended above water, with crates for seats and footsteps of the thriving nightlife above. But if there was a nook, an unused space, a seemingly pointless alleyway, Melbourne would find a way to put a café or a bar there.

He'd missed that when he was in New York, though not as much as he'd missed a certain feisty blonde.

A flash of emerald silk caught his attention. Elise sat perched on a stool with a drink in her hand, behind her the lights of the city dazzled in winking shades of yellow and orange. The green of her dress shone against creamy, bare skin. He had a weakness for her in that colour, and he'd told her so frequently. There was something about green in any shade that caused her skin to glow as if she were a naked flame.

The dress hugged her curves but draped modestly where it counted; a small side split in the knee-length skirt taunted him with a sliver of thigh. Her hair was carelessly piled on her head, the river breeze ruffling it out of formation, and two emerald-coloured stones hung from her ears.

'You're late,' she said, a half-empty cocktail in front of her. 'Later than when you originally rang.'

'I'm worth the wait.' He dropped down to the stool next to her and motioned for the bartender.

'Hardly,' she said, but the flicker of her tongue against the corner of her glossy pink lips gave her away. That tongue had given her away before.

Col fought the urge to dip his head to hers and pull her tongue into his mouth. This was supposed to be about business. An unexpected wave of guilt rocked in his stomach—so much for all those journos who said he was cold as a New York winter. He still had the capacity to know when he was doing wrong by someone.

'You look amazing.' Okay, so maybe some of it *wasn't* about business.

The corners of her lips pulled up into a forced smile. 'Are you going to tell me why you dragged me out here?'

'Why don't we catch up first?' He accepted the tumbler of soda water from the bartender. He didn't need any alcohol affecting his judgement tonight, not when Elise seemed to do that so effectively on her own. 'It's been a while. What have you been doing with yourself?'

'I've been keeping busy.' She sipped from the edge of her glass delicately, her eyes fluttering closed as she savoured the liquid. He'd brought her here because he knew for a fact that they made a good Manhattan.

Part of him was comforted by the fact that her favourite drink hadn't changed. She shifted on the bar stool and her dress moved, exposing more of her slender thigh. A gold anklet winked at him from the delicate joint of her ankle; he had an almost uncontrollable urge to run his tongue along the length of it. *Enough!*

'Seriously, tell me what's happened since I left. I'm interested.'

'In the last five years?'

'Has it been that long?' Funny how half a decade could pass when you were sticking your head in the sand.

'It most certainly has.'

'And we're both now responsible adults and entrepreneurs.'

She scoffed. 'I would hardly call myself an entrepreneur, especially around you.'

'You're running your own business, doing well for yourself.'

'And if by doing well for myself you mean running my business into the ground...' She frowned, tipping her head back to enjoy the last mouthful of her drink.

'The GFC has been rough on everyone, Ellie. Don't be so hard on yourself.'

'Sure looks like it affected you. Do you have to fly

Economy now?' Sarcasm was her defence of choice, another thing that hadn't changed.

He drew his mouth into a line. She wasn't going to make it easy for him, that was for sure. But he always found himself attracted to her ferocious will. Besides, having her at arm's length would be a good thing. He couldn't afford to get too emotionally tangled with Elise Johnson. The woman had a way of breaking his heart without even trying, and Lord knew he had enough emotional baggage when it came to rejection.

'So what have you been doing with *yourself,* Mr Forbes Young Rich List?' She gestured to the bartender to bring her another drink. A river cruise boat drifted past them.

He grunted. 'God, I *hate* that label.'

'You should be proud. The Old Rich List is so passé.' Her voice was teasing but there was a hard glint in her twilight eyes.

He cringed. 'You know I don't keep up with trends... unless they involve a circuit board, that is.'

'Seems to me like you managed to use your status to have a little fun after you moved.'

'How so?' He frowned, instinct telling him he was about to walk into a trap.

'I happened to be reading the paper a while ago and saw a rather compromising photo of you and the daughter of a certain rival technologist.'

Ah, so they were back to this again. Despite what the gossip columnists made out, Col usually ensured any 'itches that needed to be scratched' were done so with the utmost discretion. No supermodels, movie stars or society darlings for him. Until he met heiress Tessa Bates, though she had been going under a false name on the night he met her. She turned out to be rebelling against her father and had scouted Col out on one of his ultra-rare public appearances. He'd walked straight into her trap and now there were pictures of him naked on her supposedly private balcony that would haunt him for the rest of his days.

'You seem rather preoccupied with my sex life.' He attempted to redirect the conversation.

'Hardly,' she scowled.

'Well, that's the second time you've mentioned it in as many meetings.' He leant forward on his stool, his knees knocking against hers.

She stiffened. 'Who you sleep with is up to you.'

'Well, it was a mistake in any case.' He shrugged as though it bothered him less than it did.

'What about you? Are you seeing anyone?'

She pondered his question for a moment. 'No. I don't have time for messing around at the moment.'

'I thought you told me all work and no play made for a dull existence.'

She wrinkled her pert, upturned nose and changed the topic. 'So tell me, what is it that you think I can help you with?'

'That's it? After five years you give me a two-minute catch-up?'

'It was hardly two minutes.' She shrugged, unflinching. 'But it's more than you deserve.'

Col drew a long breath; he'd known this moment would come. The one where he'd need to open himself up and admit something that had plagued him since childhood. For someone who'd worked with the toughest investors in the world, the sharpest minds in the technology industry and the most vulture-like journalists, he shouldn't have any fears left. But he did. This one was buried so deep that it had rooted itself into the core of who he was. It was unshakable, unsurpassable. And he needed to confess it to Elise, the one person left in the world that he still admired.

'I have a very important event coming up, a conference.' He cleared his throat and took a sip of his drink. 'I've been invited to be the keynote speaker and I need to give a presentation on the way technology is shaping the fitness industry.'

She shook her head slowly. 'I don't know why you think I can help you out with *that*.'

'I need someone to help me prepare for the speech, not in terms of the speech itself but in terms of getting up on stage in front of all those people.' Even saying the words sent a trickle of ice-cold fear down his spine. 'You've performed your whole life. You know how to deal with the nerves, the stage fright...'

'Are you seriously telling me you're frightened of public speaking? You, Col Hillam, CEO, New York lady-killer, technological *wunderkind*, are afraid of an audience?' She rolled her eyes.

Heat crawled up his neck. It was hard enough to admit that he was afraid of something, especially when she stared at him open-mouthed like that. Anger prickled the back of his neck, making his fingers curl around his glass.

'We're all afraid of something, Elise.'

'Yes, but you're...' She threw her hands up in the air, grappling for words. 'Don't you broker deals all the time? Don't you spend your life networking and selling your business?'

If only. He was known as something of a recluse in

the industry. He could handle meetings, of course, but he avoided networking whenever he could…especially the personal kind. In fact, this was the first time he'd sat in a bar with a woman in… He couldn't even remember the last time he'd been on a date. *Not that this is a date,* he corrected himself, shoved the thought aside.

'It's different.' He squeezed the glass so hard he thought it might shatter. Forcing out a breath, he put the glass down and placed both hands on his knees, a technique he often used when he was feeling out of his depth. Perhaps he should have ordered something stronger than soda water after all.

'How is it different?' She seemed…suspicious. Did she think this was a ploy so he could get close to her?

'Being in a boardroom with ten people is fine, I can handle that. I know what I'm doing. I go hard, I'm aggressive and I win. But being up there with all those eyes watching while they wait for you to make a mistake…' His chest clenched, his breath came faster.

Wow, Col Hillam was actually scared of something. His chest rose and fell, the muscles pressing against the thin cotton of his lightweight blue shirt. His neck corded with each inhalation, lips pressed tight together, jaw clenched.

At first she'd wondered if this was his way of forcing her to spend time with him. Perhaps it was some made-up scenario that allowed him to get close to her without committing to anything. It seemed likely, since fleeing the country was his MO. But the light beading of sweat along his hairline and the white-knuckled grip he had on the rustic wooden table in front of them told a different story.

'I'm sure you could afford someone who specialised in public-speaking phobias to help you—'

'No.'

He barked the word out, drawing curious stares from the couples around them. Elise tilted her head, watching as his eyes narrowed. He was even more striking since he'd lost the youthful fullness in his face. The slopes and curves had been replaced by hard angles and sharp edges. A faint smattering of dark hair peeked out of the open collar of his shirt, the pushed-up sleeves revealing strong arms. Even his eyes looked harder; their faded blue—like worn denim—was hiding something.

'You're doing yourself a disservice, Col. Get some professional help. I'm just a ballerina.'

'You're the only one who can help me.'

He reached out and grabbed her hand, squeezing it, his thumb tracing the ridges of her knuckles. Her breath stuck in her throat as she looked at him. The furrowed brow, the serious eyes, the grim slash of a mouth were all too familiar.

'You're the only one who knows me well enough to help me get around this problem.'

Memories flooded her; she'd managed to shut them out for so long but they came roaring back when he touched her. Ten-year-old Col on her doorstep, arms black and blue with bruises, face set into a hard mask of fury. No tears; there were never any tears. He'd asked if he could stay the night and she'd let him in without a word. He'd stunk of the alcohol his father had splashed on him. She'd held him until they both fell asleep, till her father found them lying in front of the fireplace the next morning. She was the only one allowed to comfort him, the only one he'd allow within touching distance.

Even Elise's brother, Rich, who'd been Col's best friend since kindergarten, wasn't allowed that close.

'I can't help you.' The memories swirled, unsteadying her.

He gritted his teeth. 'Please, Ellie.'

She couldn't fix people that were broken; she'd learnt that the hard way. She tried and tried and tried, but eventually they either left or retreated so far into themselves that she might as well have been alone. The last time she'd tried to help Col she'd failed, and then he'd left. She was now trying in vain to drag her mother down from the brink of oblivion on a daily basis. She wouldn't put herself in that position again.

'I'm sorry, you'll need to find someone else. I'm not the right person to help you.' She shoved aside the empty cocktail glass and grabbed her bag from the table.

Weaving through the crowd, she dodged the waitress with a tray full of drinks and the other patrons until she found the staircase that led up to the bridge. When the night air hit her burning cheeks she sighed with relief. Distance, that was what she needed. If she could avoid Col while he was in Australia then everything would be fine.

CHAPTER THREE

HOW WAS SHE going to make it work? It was the less scary of the two questions Elise had been asking herself, the other being: how had she let it get to this point in the first place? She knew the answer to that: she was weak. She was too weak to say no to her mother, too weak to tell her brother to come home and face his responsibilities. She was supposed to be the stable one in the family, the reliable one. She was the one who had to keep them *all* afloat.

Elise crunched the numbers again, tapping at her calculator and hoping for a different result. The only way the numbers would balance was if she let go one of her teachers and took on more lessons herself. It wasn't ideal, but it was better than letting the business fail even more than it already had.

Sitting behind the small desk in the waiting room of the studio, she watched the mothers chatter amongst themselves while the under-twelve class finished up. The girls bounded out of the studio, full of beans despite a gruelling technique class with Jasmine. She couldn't let Jasmine go; they'd been best friends since they were six and had seen each other through many a dark day. She sighed, raking a hand through her loose hair.

'See you next Thursday, girls. Don't forget to stretch!' Jasmine chirped and waved as her students left.

Elise envied Jasmine and her newfound life with her hunky AFL star fiancé. Their kind of happiness was rare, and her best friend deserved every second of it… but she couldn't help wishing that she had a little bit of that luck too.

Swinging her sneakered feet onto the desk, she adjusted the portable fan so it blew in her direction. The studio's air conditioning was broken again, but she was trying to figure out how to afford a service. No solution had presented itself, but there was a number of blisteringly hot days in next week's forecast that meant she'd have to make a decision, and fast.

'Have you heard from Col again?' Jasmine stripped off her leg warmers and ballet shoes, before stuffing her stockinged feet into a pair of flats.

She'd neglected to tell Jasmine they'd gone for a drink last night. She wouldn't approve and Elise couldn't deal with a lecture at this point. She'd hardly slept. Between the old memories resurfacing and the stress of trying to decide which teacher to fire, relaxation and slumber were impossible concepts. There had also been a tiny twinge of guilt over bailing on Col when he'd opened up for her, but she soothed that guilt with a healthy dose of anger. He was the one who left her originally, and not just for a night…for five long years.

'Hey.' Jasmine's face appeared in front of hers, a hand landing on her shoulder. 'I'm worried about you.'

'I'm fine.' She forced a perky smile. 'You know what my apartment is like. It gets so hot in the summer. I could barely catch a wink of sleep last night.'

'Right. Well, you let me know if you want to talk.'

Jasmine removed her hand and gave her a pointed look that said: *I'm your best friend, don't BS me.*

'As if you could stop me talking.' She sat up, shaking off her exhaustion, and kept her smile firmly in place.

As Jasmine was about to leave, the door to the studio swung open. Col's frame filled the doorway almost completely, his broad shoulders looking even wider with the fading light outlining him. He wore an intense expression, none of his usual cockiness present in the deep stare he gave her.

'Hi, Ellie.'

'Col.'

Jasmine looked from Elise to Col and back again. She moved closer to the desk, hovering by Elise, looking as if she were about to strike.

'It's all right, Mama Bear,' Elise said with a nod. 'I can take him.'

She frowned. 'I'll stay if you need moral support.'

'It's fine, go.' Elise gave her friend a gentle shove with one sneaker-covered foot.

Jasmine picked up her bag and walked past Col, setting a hard glare at him before she left without a word. Elise stifled a smile, Jasmine was nothing if not fiercely loyal.

'Not a fan, I see.' Col came forward, crossing the small room in only a few strides.

'Makes two of us,' she said, trying to keep her teasing light though it sounded loaded as a drawn weapon. 'Maybe I should start a Facebook group.'

He wore a pair of fitted jeans, which were beginning to fray at both knees, a white T-shirt that looked so good it should have been illegal and a pair of black Chucks. His dark hair was unstyled, curling at the edges where

normally it would be tamed into place with hair product. A thick, leather cuff on his right wrist offset tanned
skin. He'd been outside; she could see the sunshine on
him. He was too delicious for words and she hated her
body for every traitorous reaction it was having.

'No need to be hostile.'

'What do you want, Col?'

'I want you to reconsider.'

He leant against the desk, his scent making her
heady. Faded aftershave mixed with sun-drenched skin,
a hint of cinnamon and something else…something entirely male.

'Have you forgotten our chat last night?' She forced
her eyes away from his chest. 'I gave you my answer
already. Twice now, if memory serves me correctly.'

'So you'll let this studio fail to spite me?' He leant
forward, brows crinkled. 'We can help each other.'

'I don't want your help.'

'That might be true, but you do *need* my help.'

Without the buttoned shirt, the dress trousers and
the expensive shoes he looked…normal. Just like the
boy she remembered from the night she lost her heart,
the night she came undone so badly she'd never been
able to piece herself back together. A night of muffled
cries, sweat-drenched skin and a passion so intense
she'd never been able to replicate it. In fact the last few
attempts had fallen so far short she'd about given up.

He stared down at her, his eyes making her skin
flame. 'You *could* get rid of one of your teachers,' he
went on. 'Which one? I know you won't get rid of Jasmine—she's too good a friend. What about the redhead,

Missy? You've known her forever too. Could you really put *her* out of a job? Or there's that other girl—'

'Stop it!' The cry sprang from her with such fury that Col stopped midsentence.

He closed his mouth, quietly assessing her. Her heart pounded a staccato-like beat, the throbbing in her head matching its pace. She felt as if she were about to explode from the stress, the sleeplessness, the frustration. A confused knot of emotion swelled within her, threatening to burst forth with the slightest provocation.

'You can't come back here and manipulate me into helping you,' she said through gritted teeth. 'You don't get to do that to me. *You* were the one who left.'

You were the one who ruined everything.

Col's eyes clouded over, his mouth pulling into a thin line. He pushed up from the desk and turned so he was facing her dead on. His hands landed on the desk's surface with a hard thud, his face inches from hers. She could see the rolling storm cloud of emotion in his eyes; the passionate anger, the five-year stockpile of guilt, the desire to fight.

'I did you a favour in leaving, Elise. I did us *both* a favour.'

'Bull.' She dragged her eyes away, wishing for a moment that he would give up on her.

'I promise if you help me I'll make sure your ballet studio never suffers again. I'll make sure *you* never suffer again, and I will stay well out of your life.'

For a moment he wondered if she might hold her ground. He knew she must hate him for leaving—hell, he hated himself for leaving—but that didn't change the fact that it was the best thing for them both. Her family had taken him in and he'd promised her brother that he'd never lay a hand on her...except he did. In fact he'd laid both hands, his mouth and everything else he possessed on her. It had been the best night of his life...but boy had he paid. He'd lost his best friend and thrown the kindness the Johnson family had shown him back in their faces.

Since then he kept things casual, *always* casual. One-night stands were the preference, though occasionally he let it stretch on to a second or third night. But never longer than that. No one would ever compare to her, so what was the point in trying?

But there was no way he could let history repeat itself. He wasn't hanging around and he didn't want to hurt her. That kind of mistake wouldn't happen twice.

'Strictly business,' she said. 'I don't want you trying anything funny.'

'You have my word.' The tension melted out of his muscles, his shoulders dropping down to their normal position.

She sighed. 'I still don't think I'm the right person to help you with this.'

'You are.' He nodded. 'I'm sure of it.'

'Fine, let's meet tomorrow to go over the details and then you can tell me what it is you think I can do.' She waved a hand as if to dismiss him. 'I've got to get home.'

'Tomorrow it is. We could meet for breakfast?' He knew she had a weakness for bacon and eggs. Perhaps her favourite food might help her ease into the idea of working with him.

'The old place we used to go on Saturdays.' A glimmer of a smile crossed her lips.

'The one with the green eggs.'

She nodded.

He got to the café early, though he told himself it was nothing to do with securing the private little booth down the back. He was a morning person, so it made sense to arrive early. *Totally rational behaviour.*

He put in a call to his office, spoke with his executive assistant and his second in charge. Everything seemed to be running smoothly without him, which was exactly what he demanded when he left. The details for his keynote speech had been locked down; his communications person had already started working on the research to back up his presentation. Everything was swimming along.

Now all he had to do was deal with the not so little problem of his public-speaking phobia. Baby steps—the first thing he needed to do was get Elise to give him some insights into her performance preparation. Then he could figure out which tactics would work for him, and figure out how to practise them in a close-to-real-life scenario. It was how he tackled all of his problems: find someone who was good at what he wanted to do, learn as much as he could, practise over and over, execute.

He was one of those businessmen who believed firmly in surrounding himself with the very best people his money could buy. Elise was no exception.

'Morning.' Elise's voice pulled him into the present. She slid into the booth across from him, looking about as stunning as one could so early in the morning. Her golden hair was in disarray, the wispy strands fanning out around her shoulders, kinked in places from sleep. She wore denim shorts and a boldly printed top with straps so thin they looked as though they would break with the slightest tug. A long gold chain hung down past her breasts, weighted by a small gold fan, and he knew without even looking that she'd have that delicate anklet around one slender ankle. Against his will, his heart kicked up a notch.

'You're looking very spritely,' he replied, taking a sip of his macchiato and forcing himself not to admire the smooth expanse of skin the summery outfit offered up like a gift from the heavens.

'And if by spritely you mean I rolled out of bed and happened to land on these clothes…then, yes,' she drawled, smiling up at the waiter as he came to take their order.

The café was small with their booth offering additional privacy against the other breakfast-goers. They'd spent many a Saturday morning here when Col had first got his licence. He was living with Elise and her family then, and he tried to repay his debts by helping out as much as possible. One of the ways he did that was by ferrying Elise to her ballet lessons on the weekend; they would always come early so she could carb load for a long day of training.

Those breakfasts with her were the highlight of his week. She'd been oblivious to how he felt about her back then, too busy being a bun-head with her sights firmly set on ballet-world domination. How things had changed…

'So, let's get down to business,' she said, pulling a

notebook and pen from her bag. She'd come prepared, clearly with the goal of ensuring he stayed true to his word about it being a business-only engagement. 'What is it you think you want from me?'

'I told you, I need help preparing for a speech.'

'How about some details, Col? Because from here I feel like you're barking up the wrong tree.'

He drew a breath. 'I need some insights into your preparation for going out on stage, what you do for nerves, how you relax and that kind of stuff.'

She looked at him strangely. 'I'm usually stretching up against a wall before going on stage, not doing breathing exercises.'

He knew exactly what she looked like when she stretched; he'd spent many a night growing up trying to ignore the insane flexibility she had. He'd mastered the art of peripheral vision so as not to alert her brother or parents to the fact that he couldn't keep his eyes off her. It was not an image he needed in his mind right now. Thinking about that would only lead him to feeling like a horny teenager again.

He shoved the thought aside and ignored the clenching in his stomach. 'I'm talking about the mental preparation. Breathing exercises, meditation, feng shui… whatever.'

'I don't know, I kind of slip straight into it…' She shook her head.

'Come on, Elise. You know damn well there's more to it than that, I saw you practising all the time when we were growing up. You *can* help me.'

His voice had an edge of desperation that irritated him beyond belief. God, how he hated not having the upper hand. But he knew that going in aggressive was *not* the way to convince Elise to do something; the second she thought someone was backing her into a corner she'd come out fighting like a kung-fu ninja. He'd borne the wounds of that particular mistake before.

'Fine,' she said, throwing her hands up. 'What else?'

'I want you to help me prepare for the presentation *and* I want you to be there when I deliver it.'

'You want me to be in the audience?' Her brows arched and she tilted her head. 'Why?'

'Because I know I'll need it.'

He shifted in his seat. Col was about as far out of his comfort zone as he could possibly be. Talking about his weaknesses was generally a no-go area; normally when he hired great people to take care of the different aspects of his business it didn't involve him talking about any personal failings. His palms itched, his leg bounced an uneven beat. He was ready to run, ready to call the conference organisers and tell them that he couldn't do the speech. It would be easier.

No, you're not a quitter. You're not *a failure.*

'It's non-negotiable,' he said, squaring his shoulders and slipping into work mode. 'You have to be there on the day, otherwise there's no point to this deal.'

She contemplated his demands, plucking at a strand of her golden hair and twirling it around her finger. Her tongue flickered out to the corner of her mouth. She was close to agreeing; he could feel it.

'Any other deal breakers I should be aware of?'

'No.'

Their breakfast arrived and Col tucked into his scrambled eggs with gusto. Perhaps if he kept his senses busy with a delicious breakfast, he could stop thinking about the past…stop remembering.

'What about you?' He speared a piece of bacon. 'Don't you want to know how much I'm going to pay you?'

'Your generosity has never been in question, Col.' Her voice softened, the defensiveness seeping out of her posture. 'I know you're a fair man.'

He couldn't handle her when she went all soft on him. That made her *far* too tempting. 'That's poor business practice, you know. Perhaps you need to be a little less trusting when it comes to money—might be better for the studio.' He gestured towards her with his fork.

She bristled. 'It's different when I'm dealing with you. I don't trust anyone else, I'm not stupid.'

She trusted him? Even after he'd left her, she still trusted him? That was far too confusing a thought to process, so he shook his head and forced himself to stick to business.

'I know you're not stupid, Elise, but it worries me that someone will take advantage of you.'

'How about some of my requirements?' she said, changing the subject.

'Shoot.'

'I don't want you to thank me.' Her chin jutted forward, a serious look clouding her usual expression of elfin mischief.

He raised a brow. 'What do you mean by that?'

'You're paying me. I don't owe you anything after it's over, and you don't owe me. We're square, even, *finito.*'

The fact that she was already thinking about the end of their deal cut him deeper than he wanted it to. 'Fine. What else?'

'If you want my help then I don't expect any attitude if I push you to do things that aren't comfortable.

I don't accept it from my ballet students, so I won't accept it from you.'

He nodded. It seemed fair; he wouldn't accept anything less of himself.

'Last thing, we keep our focus.' She dragged her lower lip between her teeth, pausing as if figuring out the correct words to use. 'I don't want to talk about the past, I don't want to ask any questions and I don't want you to give me any answers.'

His chest ached as if a great, big gaping chasm had split it in two. She wanted to forget that she'd practically saved his life, that she was an integral part of who he was…what he'd become. *Suck it up, you left* her. *Deal with it.*

'Okay?' She stretched the word out, her grey eyes fixed on him.

'Okay.'

She nodded, satisfied. 'Then I'll help you.'

Relief flooded through him. 'I'll have my legal adviser draft up a contract with the terms of our agreement and outline how much I'm willing to pay for your services.'

'Fine.' She waved her hand to dismiss him.

Clearly 'keeping focus' didn't include talking financials. He rubbed a hand along his jaw, studying her until she caught his steady gaze.

'I still find all this strange, you know. I mean, haven't you done interviews and press conferences before?'

He should have. He'd sold his first computer application at twenty-two, subsequently creating and then selling a start-up company to a technology giant just three years later. He'd been the youngest person to make a million dollars off a company that was less than a year old—though the record had now been broken by a pair of sixteen-year-olds from California.

There had been a lot of media interest at the time of the sale, but he'd staunchly refused interviews and it had become something of a distinguishing feature as his career had grown. One paper had gone so far as to label him 'the CEO hermit'. In many ways, he knew it was bad for his career to be so media-shy…and this conference was his opportunity to prove to himself that he could conquer his fears. That he was taking steps towards greater success. That he'd moved on from being the charity case he was in school.

'I tend to focus on what's important, and that's building innovative technology.' He shoved another forkful of eggs into his mouth. 'Not hamming it up for the press. This conference, however, is a great opportunity for my company…so I'm going to do it.'

A cold drip of fear trickled down his spine. Thinking about hundreds of eyes being locked onto him while he stood on stage, the lone occupant of a bright spotlight, was enough to make his chest compress in on itself. His breath became shallow, the muscles in his neck stiffening. Suddenly his breakfast didn't seem so appealing.

'I guess you always were a bit of an introvert growing up,' she conceded, bobbing her head. 'You were always fiddling with your computers, playing video games. I guess all your passions were indoor activities.'

He didn't bother to argue; the reason he'd started tinkering with computers in the first place was because he needed something to do to pass the time while his bruises were at their most prominent. Wrinkling his nose, he pushed his plate away from him. He needed to change the topic. Fast.

'You even helped me indulge some of those indoor activities.' He made no effort to hide the teasing in his voice.

A flicker of emotion passed over her face, gone as quickly as it appeared. She pushed her breakfast around her plate with her fork; she'd barely touched it. 'Must be a different life now, having to deal with so many people instead of being holed up on your own.'

'It is,' he said. 'I can't just think about myself any more. I have a team to lead. They rely on the success of the company, and I have a very big part to play.'

'I bet they look up to you.' A soft smile pulled her lips up and for a moment she was lost in her own thoughts.

'They do.'

Yes, the mask he wore for his team was a good one—solid, practised, comforting. He'd started young, putting on a brave face for the teachers, the doctors, the Johnsons. Being a leader was a learned behaviour, but to the untrained eye it appeared as natural to him as putting his clothes on in the morning. Luckily for him, no one knew what was going on inside...no one except Elise.

CHAPTER FOUR

'YOU AGREED TO do what I said.' Elise planted her hands on her hips and tried to stifle the curve of a wicked smile on her lips.

Two flint-like blue eyes stared back at her with such an intensity she could have sworn they were about to fire lightning bolts at her. Col's breath came rapidly, his chest rising and falling within the confines of his grey T-shirt. Muscles bulged as he crossed his arms tight across his chest.

She stood her ground, staunchly refusing to look at how incredible his body was. It was those biceps; they were a damn distraction!

'This is ridiculous and pointless and...*cruel*.' He looked at the group of little girls who were bouncing up and down on the spot, amusing themselves by babbling to one another and trying to point their ballet-slippered feet.

'If you can't stand to be in front of a group of four-year-olds, who don't understand the concept of judgement, then how can you get up in front of a room full of your peers or your competitors?'

'This is absolute bull—'

Elise silenced him with a look.

'Bull…poop.' He glared at her. 'And you *know* it.'

Okay, so perhaps sticking Col at the front of her class full of four-year-old ballet students had the benefit of personal amusement. But she had warned him: if he wanted her help then she was in charge. End of story.

'If you no longer require my services feel free to leave.' She held her hand out to the door, calling his bluff.

'What about the mothers?' He gestured to the viewing window where several of the students' mothers milled around, watching the class and talking amongst themselves. 'Would they really want a man in here with their kids?'

She smiled sweetly, relishing having the upper hand for once. 'Oh, I got their permission. They're totally fine with it.'

Defeated, he gritted his teeth and squared his shoulders, facing the class. *Good boy.*

'Okay, class,' she began in her best teacher voice. 'Today we have a special guest joining us. This is my friend, Col, and I want you to make him feel very welcome. He's going to be helping me run the lesson today.'

One of her students jabbed a chubby finger in Col's direction, her cherubic face pulled into a suspicious scowl. 'You don't *look* like a ballet teacher. Where are your ballet shoes?'

Elise's eyes dropped to the floor. Col's bare feet stuck out from the frayed hems of his worn jeans. He rocked up onto the balls of his feet so that his heels left the floor. Her eyes travelled back up, skimming over the denim that hugged his muscular thighs like a second skin. His T-shirt was fitted, tight enough to hint at the perfection beneath but not tight enough to look self-serving.

Col shrugged. 'I'm starting a trend.'

The little girl peered at him and then seemed to accept his answer, turning her face to Elise as if to say: *okay, you can start now.*

'We're going to start with our *tendus*.' Elise clapped her hands together to get the attention of her class, most of whom were more interested in twirling on the spot than completing the set exercises. 'Ready, one, two...'

She started the music and stepped her students through the exercise, stifling a laugh as Col bumbled along beside her. He tried to keep in time with the music, but the sad fact was he had about as much musicality as a stuffed llama.

Okay, so maybe this *was* cruel and unusual...but didn't she deserve to have a little fun? Her life was sorely lacking in the good F-word of late...actually, it had been sorely lacking in the other kind of F-word as well, and Col's sudden arrival had spun her out. Between sifting through the confusing emotions associated with his return, she had a failing business to save and a mother with mental-health demands that would test even the most Zen of people.

'Miss Johnson, you're messing up the steps!'

She shook her head, stopping the music so they could start again. A heavy hand came down on her shoulder; the flint in Col's eyes had been replaced by something else...something that made her insides feel gooey.

'Sorry girls...and boy.' Her cheeks burned and she moved out from under Col's touch. 'Even teachers mess up the steps sometimes.'

'Why don't we try it again?' The little girl used the phrase she often said when her line of little angels fell into distraction.

'Great idea, Ginny.'

Elise fumbled with the remote, suddenly off balance and feeling a little dizzy. Maybe it was something she'd had at lunch…had she even *eaten* lunch? Or breakfast, for that matter?

'Whoa there.' Col stepped in close and held her as the ground swam beneath her feet. 'Elise?'

His arms held her tight, the space between them closed far too quickly for her to think, to react. His cinnamon and wood scent engulfed her, making her sway in his arms. Oh, no, this could *not* be happening.

'Miss Johnson! Miss Johnson!' The students called her name as Elise's eyelids fluttered closed.

'I'm okay.' She pressed a palm to her head and tried to steady herself, nudging herself away from Col's grip with her elbow.

'You're white as a sheet.'

'I'm *fine*.' She took a step and the room tilted around her sharply, as though someone had tipped the ballet studio over like a child's playing block.

'Yeah, I'll believe that when you can stand on your own.' Col pulled her around his neck. 'Come on, let's find you a seat.'

They walked over to the front of the studio where her MP3 player and stereo system were kept. She settled into the small plastic chair and dropped her head into her hands. If only the room would stop spinning…

'Are you okay?'

He slowly peeled her hands away from her face, his touch sending shock waves through her system. Each time he touched her it was as if her body were reignited with memories, the images flickering, sounds, gasps, the taste of his skin under her lips. *No!*

'I'm just a little dizzy.'

'When was the last time you ate?' His dark brows crinkled.

'Afternoon tea…' She wasn't sure if she should read anything into the fact that he remembered her tendency to skip meals when she was stressed. She looked up. 'Yesterday.'

'Dammit, Elise.' He growled the words and shook his head. 'You *have* to take care of yourself.'

At that moment Jasmine came jogging in, a long floating skirt swirling around her legs as she moved. 'Girls, I want you all to practise your *tendus* for me. The best *tendu* will get a prize after class.'

The group of tiny ballerinas attempted a few steps on their own before descending into giggling chaos.

'What's going on?' Jasmine's brows pulled together. 'Do you need me to take over the class?'

Elise nodded mutely.

'Someone has decided that calorific intake is an optional part of her day.' Col folded his arms across his chest.

'Ellie!' Jasmine scowled.

'Oh, don't you give me any crap.' Elise held up her hand in warning. 'What were you like when you were fighting with lover boy a few months back?'

'Leave the class with me,' Jasmine said, looking behind her and ordering the students back into position. Her wary gaze hovered on Col momentarily, while she figured out whether or not to trust him. 'Can you take her to get some food? And make sure she eats it—don't leave it with her. Watch *every* mouthful.'

'You have my word.'

Jasmine rounded up the students and set about conducting the class in her long skirt and bare feet. Taking a deep breath, Elise got up from the chair but her arms wobbled and Col had to help her stand. She closed her eyes, forcing away the swishing sensation in her head.

'When did you get so skinny?' he said, his large hand around her upper arm as she steadied herself. 'I feel like I'm holding a chicken bone.'

'Don't start.'

She was a nervous under-eater. Whereas some people reached for chips and chocolate when they were upset, Elise felt ill at the sight of any and all food. It wasn't as if she habitually starved herself; she just couldn't stomach anything in times of stress. Was it her fault that those times were frequent these days?

'Hey.' Col's hand came to her cheek, brushing back a strand of her hair behind her ear. 'I'm worried about you, Ellie-girl.'

'You're a little too late for that.' The lack of food was making her emotional; she could feel the pain simmering beneath the surface, churning her stomach and making her heart thump. Luckily for her she was unable to cry, and that meant she could keep herself in check.

She shrugged herself out of Col's grip and walked through the studio, behind the class, and avoided Jasmine's gaze as she left. She waved a quick goodbye to the mothers without stopping; the last thing she needed was anyone asking questions.

'This is karma, you know.' Col followed her outside.

The last rays of sunshine threw golden light around the ballet studio car park as the glowing giant orb dipped in the distance. How was it that she was suddenly noticing the weather, the inherent beauty of summer, when normally she rushed to her car without giving the view a second glance?

She shook off the strange thoughts. 'Karma?'

'Yeah, for your silly lesson tonight.'

A smile tugged on the corner of her lips. She'd rather have him joking with her than pitying her. Joking was squarely in the realms of her comfort zone along with its good friends denial and repression.

'Col, you're paying me for my expertise. Why don't you let me handle the lesson planning?'

'If you try a stunt like that again I'll make you pay for it.'

She stopped at her car and he stood close to her. Awareness ran through her veins at full speed; she could hear nothing but the sound of his breath coming a little too quickly, the scrape of his palm across his stubble-covered jaw. She could swear she heard his heartbeat, or perhaps it was the insistent thumping of her own. Like many times before she failed to see where she ended and he began.

Elise turned to him with a slow movement carefully designed not to upset her delicate balance. Her cheeks were stained rose-pink, her grey eyes hooded by dark lashes. The urge to kiss her roared in him at full force, his weakness for her as unsettlingly brilliant now as it had been all those years ago. He'd never met another girl like her, not a one that could compare to the layers of maddening complexity and uniqueness that drew him to her like a magnet. She was fiercely indepen-dent and yet he knew that beneath the sarcasm and the joking and the flippancy there was a vulnerability so precious and beautiful he would have given everything to have a taste.

He *had* given everything for a taste once; he'd broken a promise to his best friend and paid for it with everything he had. But something now told him that he'd do it all over again. He'd give up all he had for her over and over. *Snap out of it—that ship has sailed. You lost it all last time and leaving her was the right thing to do.*

'And how exactly will you make me pay?' She tipped her nose up at him, all bravado and temptation.

He leant down so that his lips were near her ear. 'You don't want to find out.'

He felt the shiver that ran through her even though there was still a sliver of space between them. He noticed the flare of her pupils, the quick intake of breath, and the way her tongue darted out the side of her mouth. That tongue was going to bring him undone.

'I think you're all talk and no action, Colby Hillam.'

'Elise...' he growled in warning.

'All. Talk.' She sounded the words out slowly, her lips wrapping around the taunt in a way that sent fire through his blood. 'No. Action.'

Before his sensibilities had the chance to act, he grabbed her by the shoulders and pressed her up against the car with a gentle thud. His face hovered inches from hers, so close that he could see the faded freckles that ran across her nose and the strange little ring of gold that stopped her eyes from being *just* grey.

Her lips parted in response, though whether it was from shock or invitation he didn't know. The front of his trousers was so tight that he yearned to press against her, to relieve the pressure, to drown himself in pleasure. Her lashes touched together and she stayed still as a statue. He could kiss her, he could drop his head and plunder that sweet, delicious mouth of hers so damn easily…

Don't you lose it, don't you dare.

'I'm taking you to dinner.' He stepped back, holding his shoulders square and ignoring the aching dissatisfaction that made his limbs heavy and wooden.

She rolled her eyes. 'Gee, when you invite me so politely like that, how could I refuse?'

'Such a smart mouth on such an angelic-looking face.' He shook his head. 'And I know for a fact that "polite" doesn't work with you.'

She opened her mouth to protest when her stomach growled loudly. 'Fine, but I'm driving.'

After a quick trip they were seated in a small Italian restaurant…emphasis on the *small*. From the outside it had looked like a family restaurant, a safe zone for him to keep his mind on appropriate topics like her performance preparation. Now that they were seated, the warm glow of a candle softened the light, bringing out the gold tones in her hair, and their knees bumped in the intimate space. And Col did not feel very safe at all.

So far during his time in Australia he'd accomplished little. He'd delayed on cleaning out his father's house because he couldn't stand the sight of the place; he'd scarcely looked over the speaking notes his communications person had sent him, and used all that wasted time battling thoughts he shouldn't be having. Thoughts about all he'd given up when he left.

'Don't try and pull another stunt like you did tonight,' Col said, forcing his mind onto how ticked off he was supposed to be.

'It wasn't a stunt. I was merely simulating a stage

atmosphere.' She tore a piece of garlic bread in two and chewed on one half. 'Just because it happened to hold some personal amusement doesn't make it any less valuable a lesson.'

'Don't give me that. If there's one thing I know for sure about you, Elise, it's that you're aware of each and every little thing you do.' He took a swig of his red wine and looked at her pointedly. 'So don't play innocent with me. I'm not falling for it.'

She nodded and stifled a smile. 'Can you blame a girl for trying to get a little payback on the guy who did the adult version of a pash and dash?'

'That was your payback for me *leaving*? I thought it was for all the times I called you Bun Head.'

'I wore the Bun Head label with pride back in the day.' A wistful smile passed over her lips.

'You lived and breathed ballet.'

'It was all I ever wanted.' She circled the rim of her wineglass with a fingertip. 'Do you remember that time that I was late for rehearsal and you picked me up from work? I had to change in the back of the car because my teacher would have locked me out if I came to a lesson without my uniform.'

Did he remember? Who would forget a beautiful girl in the back seat of their car, stripping out of her work clothes and wriggling into a skimpy leotard and tights? He swallowed, the front of his trousers tightening uncomfortably again.

Guilt washed over him like a slow-moving wave. Giving in to temptation with Elise was one of the worst decisions he'd ever made. Now here he was, five years later, and still looking at her as though she were the most delicious, perfect thing in the world. Had he learned nothing?

'Fair's fair, Col. Let's talk about your presentation, no funny business this time.' She twirled a fork in her spaghetti and popped the neat forkful into her mouth.

'What, no emasculating humiliation?' he drawled. 'And here I was getting used to it.'

'No, I've had my fun.' She grinned. 'In all serious-ness, a good place to start would be to look at *why* you're scared of public speaking. This might help to work out what preparation techniques would help most.'

'I was looking more for a "breathe and count to ten" kind of approach.' He raked a hand through his hair and bounced his right leg in a rapid beat. 'The whole Dr Phil thing isn't for me.'

'If you want to be able to get up in front of all those people you need to do it. Are we talking a hundred peo-ple in the audience? A thousand?'

He felt the panic creep up his spine, the tightness close around his neck like a pair of icy hands. 'I don't know.'

He'd been avoiding that part of the brief his assis-tant put together because he knew the kind of reaction it would incite. He let out a breath; this public speaking thing was his damn Achilles heel. He wanted to thump his fist against the table, but instead he held himself rigid and still.

'Anyway, that's not important.' She waved her hand and toyed with her fork. 'Do you think it's the size of the audience? You mentioned you were okay with a boardroom, so perhaps we need to find some guinea pigs for you to practise in front of—'

'No.' It came out as a snap though he didn't mean it

that way. It was hard to speak, hard to keep his mind from doing that horrible spinning-top thing it did whenever he thought about the speech.

Elise peered at him, her face serious. 'If you can't do a practise run then how do you expect to get up there on the day?'

I don't know. It was ridiculous. A man of his success, with an innovative, ground-breaking technology company to his name and…well, that was really all he had. But it was big. Important. As far away as humanly possible from the derelict life he'd had growing up.

What the hell was he doing? He should tell the conference he had very important 'CEO business' to attend to back home and then he could leave without humiliating himself. His heart drummed, the echo bouncing around inside his body. But that would mean cutting short his time with Elise. Every fibre of his being resisted the idea of leaving her, though he knew control around her was tenuous at best.

He should leave. She didn't need someone like him around, who was all kinds of screwed up.

'Col?' Elise's voice interrupted his thoughts.

'I'm not doing it. End of story.'

'Stubborn as always, I see.'

The candle in between them flickered as if sensing the tension crackling between them. Under the table Col felt Elise's slender leg pressed against his own, and his body heated as if he'd been lowered into a hot bath.

'Like you can talk.' He stabbed a ravioli with his fork.

'I'm not stubborn.'

He thought for a moment. 'No, you're *beyond* stubborn. What would that be called? Bull-headed, perhaps?'

Her mouth formed an indignant little 'o' and blood roared in his ears. Feisty, prickly, claws-out Elise was always his favourite version of her. He felt as if that version of Elise could take on anything.

'Look, this conversation is all very interesting but you still haven't answered my question.' She was trying to get the upper hand again.

'What question?'

'The one where I asked you *why* you have such a fear of public speaking.' She watched him carefully.

'And I told *you* I didn't want to do the Dr Phil thing.' He speared another piece of pasta and then another, his fork clicking against the china plate.

'How can I help you if you won't be up-front with me? You're paying me—I would expect that you'd want your money's worth.'

The defiant glint in her eyes made his throat clench. *She* was the one who'd said she wanted to keep it strictly business, not talk of the past, no questions and answers. Elise never did well with emotion, not those that were as uncomfortable and dark as he experienced anyway. She was raised to be stoic, and now she wanted to know what blemish—of the many—on his personal history made him this way.

He sighed, deciding it would be easier to take the high road. 'Remember that time when we were kids and we had to give a presentation to homeroom on Family Day?'

Her golden brows creased; her eyes flickered as if she were flicking through the files in her memory.

'You remember, Elise. Your dad came along and you both gave a presentation on catching bad guys.'

She nodded, confusion still twisting her features while she tried to remember. 'It's all a bit vague…'

'My presentation didn't go as well as yours.' A lump lodged in his throat, the humiliation burning as brightly in his chest as it had all those years ago. 'I was worried enough about having Dad come to the school as it was. I couldn't say he was a doctor, a lawyer or a cop. He didn't help people in his job…hell, he didn't even *have* a job half the time. Then he turned up drunk.'

He watched blood drain from Elise's face. Oh, yeah, she remembered it now.

'He stumbled into the room and puked all over the floor.' Her voice was a mere whisper. 'They wanted to call child services but we ended up taking you home.'

'You let me stay there for a week.'

'And then after a while you moved in permanently.' Her eyes flickered up to him.

'*That's* why I hate public speaking. At first I'd thought he'd forgotten about Family Day and hadn't turned up like the bum he was, but then he stumbled in while I was speaking.' He swallowed. Talking about it was like slashing open an old wound that had split and healed countless times over his life.

'Everyone was looking at you. Looking at him.' He heard the catch in her voice as she processed the memory.

'Every time I get on stage all I can think about is him, ruining my presentation, showing everyone what I so desperately wanted to hide.'

'No one will ever do that to you again. He won't

hurt you anymore.' Her hands reached out to clasp his across the table.

She'd said she didn't want to talk about the past, but her eyes stared at him as though she was trying to find the answers without asking any questions. He turned his hands over so they were palm to palm.

'I know.' Col sighed. 'He's dead.'

CHAPTER FIVE

AFTER ELISE DROPPED Col back to his car she drove home, her head swimming with conflicting emotions. She was supposed to be angry at Col. After all, she was only helping him because he was paying her and she really, *really* needed the money. So why did she feel this aching compassion for him?

Was it because she'd remembered what he'd gone through growing up? Or because she knew that her one night in his arms had bound her to him forever?

She sat in the car outside her house, staring off into space. She supposed that in times of intense frustration others might cry, might scream, might release the tension. But she'd been trained to push it all down, to compact the emotions until they were tiny, dense cubes of feeling that she could swallow and hide away from the world.

Sighing, she got up from the driver's seat and swung the car door open. The balmy night air caressed her bare legs and a light breeze ruffled her hair. She swung her bag over one shoulder and headed up the stone pathway to her small town house. Gardenia trees perfumed the air with their glorious, floral scent and Elise breathed deep. She needed to get Col out of her head for good.

If only she could fast forward a few weeks until he was back in the States and she could go back to trying to piece her life together.

As she opened the front door a noise startled her. 'Hello?'

'Ellie?' A croaky voice called out.

'Mum? Is that you?' Her heart sank. If her mother was here it could only mean one thing.

She found Darlene Johnson lying on the couch, her pale face lined with the pain of the past. Dark purple rings encircled her eyes, her bony arms wrapped around her slender body. She seemed to look thinner and thinner each day.

'What are you doing here?' She dropped her bag onto the coffee table and bent down to tend to her mother.

'I couldn't sleep.'

The older woman's eyes were the exact same grey as Elise's, her nose the exact same button shape. Elise's father had always said she was a tiny replica of her mother, inside and out. Fierce, stubborn, bossy. Prone to pushing others around, loath to show weakness. At her best: a vivacious force. At her worst: an immovable object incapable of opening up.

Now her mother was an emotionless shell of a woman whose medication had hollowed her out and taken away her spark. 'Do you want to stay here tonight?'

Darlene nodded. 'I can sleep on the couch.'

'Don't be silly,' Elise said, grabbing her mother's hand and helping her to stand. 'It'll only take a second to make up the bed. Do you want a herbal tea?'

Darlene nodded again. Elise went into the kitchen and put the kettle on. She steadied herself against the countertop, massaging her temples with her fingertips.

Sometimes she wondered if she was the right person to have been left in charge of this family after their lives turned to crap. But who else would have done it?

Her mother was incapable of even the most menial tasks on her bad days, and Elise's brother Rich had bailed two years after their father died. So it was all on her shoulders to keep her mother safe and to make sure the ballet studio survived. Easy, right? She let out a breath and rolled her shoulders, trying to relax the tight muscles.

The kettle whistled and she poured the piping-hot water into an old teapot. While the tea bag steeped she made her mother a place to sleep. The old hinges of the sofa bed groaned when she unfolded them, the mattress threadbare in places. She fished the spare pillows from her hallway linen cupboard and poured two mugs of tea.

'Thanks, Ellie.' Darlene accepted the cup and sat down on the bed, shifting to avoid the patch where the hinges pushed through the mattress. 'You're a good daughter.'

Elise shifted, unused to such open praise from her mother.

'The bank called me about the loan the other day.' There was a tremor in her voice, a fear that made Elise's heart feel as if it were about to splinter.

'Yeah, they called me too.'

'What are we going to do? I haven't got much left—'

'It's fine, Mum. I'll take care of it,' she soothed.

The shakes had started; her hands trembled around the cup. The hot tea swished, slopping over the edge. 'But they said—'

'Stop worrying.' Elise used a firm tone, her hand

steadying Darlene's wrist so she didn't burn herself. 'I'll take care of it.'

'You're a good daughter,' Darlene whispered again. 'I never meant to put us in this situation. It's all my fault, it's all my fau—'

'Stop it.' She didn't want to hear the guilty pleas, the declaration of fault. She didn't want to talk about the past, not even with her own mother.

'I've stuffed everything up. I've ruined it all.'

'Stop!' There was a waver in her voice, a crack showing in her façade. She couldn't let her mother see the strain, the stress. She had to keep it locked down; she *had* to deal.

'I wish your father were still here. I wish we'd never gone on that raid…'

'You need to sleep, Mum. You're getting delirious.'

Darlene handed her barely touched tea to Elise and crawled into the sofa bed. The white sheet outlined her childlike frame. Elise set the cups down on the coffee table and put a blanket over her mother.

'Sleep tight,' she whispered, patting her mother on the arm. She had an instinct to hug her but she held back; hugging had never been a very big part of the Johnson household. 'Leave everything with me.'

Deep breathing filled the room. Peace, at last.

Rows and rows and rows of seats stretched out and up in front of him. They were empty, except for one in the centre of the front row. Elise looked at him and nodded encouragingly. He paced the stage, the sound of his shoes echoing in the silence.

'You have to get comfortable with your surroundings,' she said, standing up from her seat and walk-

ing up the steps that led onto the stage. 'Get used to
the space, know where the hazards are. Stand behind
the lectern.'

'Now?'

'Yes, now,' she said, her voice sharp, businesslike.

'Bossy boots much,' he muttered under his breath.

He'd been woken early by a phone call from Elise.
Apparently she'd had a brainwave overnight and thought
that the two of them should meet where his speech was
to be held. There was no mention of the memory he'd
shared at dinner, no questions about the audience or
the speech itself. True to her word, she didn't want to
talk about any of that. Though now it was out in the
open Col felt as if someone had unlocked the gates of
his past, and he'd tossed and turned with dreams of his
childhood all night.

'I heard that.'

'You were meant to.' He stood behind the lectern,
his hands immediately clutching it as if it were a life
raft and he were stranded at sea.

'Okay, smarty-pants. Does the mike work?'

There was an on-off switch. He pushed the button
and a green light appeared at the base of the microphone. He tapped it and the sound echoed through the
auditorium speakers.

'Check, check. One, two.'

'Very creative.'

Elise stood at the edge of the stage, one hand on her
hip. She wore a pair of jeans that were shredded up and
down the front so that enticing flashes of creamy skin
peeked through. A plain black T-shirt sat close to the
skin, highlighting her slim waist and small frame. Her
hair was plaited over one shoulder, making her look

young though not innocent, and she wore little make-up. As usual.

'Now, pretend I'm your audience. You're just talking to me, no judgement, no pressure.' She gestured with her hands, a pile of bracelets jangling as she moved.

Col unfolded the page of notes he'd printed from his makeshift office at the hotel. He smoothed the creases with his palms, trying to ignore the tremor of his hands. It was just her, Elise. It would be the first time she'd seen him exposed, raw. He could do this.

'Whereas once health and fitness was left in the hands of professionals,' he began, 'the introduction of smartphones, tablets and twenty-four-seven information has meant a dramatic shift in the way people manage their lives, health included. Technology companies have seized this opportunity, smart technology companies have used concepts like gamification to...'

He tripped over his words here and there, his breath short as the nerves tightened his chest and throat. But all the while Elise urged him on, smiling and nodding at the right points and using her hands to encourage him to keep going when he stumbled.

By the time he finished he felt as though he'd ridden a roller coaster: his stomach was fluttering; his heartbeat raced. He couldn't even contemplate how it would feel on the day with hundreds of eyes staring back at him. But it was a step in the right direction.

He moved out from behind the lectern and Elise bounced up to him, throwing her arms around his neck. 'I'm so proud of you.'

Time seemed to freeze in the moment her body pressed against him, his hands gluing themselves to her tiny waist. His whole world had suddenly shrunk to the space between them, the sound of his breath coming fast, the scent of soft flowers on her skin. She was it, the reason his heart continued to beat in those seconds, the reason he drew breath.

His hand traced a line up her arm, skating around her neck to cup the curve of her head. His fingers tangled in her hair, his thumb smoothing over the shell of her ear.

Her breath hitched, eyes fluttering. She lowered her hands from his neck until her palms were flat against his chest. 'What happened to keeping this strictly business?'

'You started it.'

She drew her bottom lip between her teeth and paused, as if deciding what to do. Her fingers fanned out, increasing the contact between them. He ached with the desire to kiss her. She shifted on the spot, brushing her pelvis against him so gently he might have imagined it. Arousal flared through him, spiralling heat down to his gut and hardening him in an instant.

'I should stop it.' Her voice cracked, colour spreading up her neck to bloom in her cheeks.

'We both should.'

He ignored his own words, lowering his head slowly to hers. Her face tilted up, lips parting. Blood roared in his ears, pulsing loud and hot and fast. She would taste so sweet, so—

A bang from the other side of the auditorium startled them and they broke apart. Cool air rushed over him, the absence of her hands on his chest like a gaping chasm in his heart.

'I didn't mean to interrupt,' the intruder said, sounding as though she didn't care at all. 'We need to set up for the next group coming through, so I'll need to ask you to wrap it up now.'

Had she almost kissed Col? Her cheeks burned, skin scorched from his touch. Worst of all, her lady parts throbbed as if they'd had a glimpse of heaven and wouldn't be quiet until they got what they wanted. She squeezed her thighs together, trying to squash the aching unfulfilled desire to no avail.

She fiddled with the end of her braid, needing desperately to occupy her hands now that they weren't pressed against Col's chest. God, she'd nearly fainted at the rock-hard muscle under her fingertips. She could only imagine how his body had morphed since she'd seen it last.

He looked utterly delectable today; he always did when he was at his most casual. Fitted jeans hugged his lean hips and curved around his perfect arse, a navy and white striped T-shirt accentuated broad shoulders and brought out the blue of his eyes. He wore his favourite sneakers, a pair of lived-in white Chucks identical to her own.

'We should get going.' His hand was at her arm, leading her to the exit.

The sunshine blinded her as they exited the conference building. The full-strength summer heat bore down reflecting off the building windows and washing everything out. She looked up to Col, shielding her eyes.

'Where to now?'

She didn't want to go home and the air conditioning still hadn't been fixed at the studio. The first half of Col's payment should be coming through shortly, but until then she was still keeping a low profile as far as her spending was concerned.

'I've got some stuff to take care of at Dad's place.' He sighed, plucking the sunglasses that hung from the neckline of his T-shirt and slipping them on. 'I need to get it done, otherwise the landlord is going to be on my case. Not that there's anything worth salvaging in there.'

'Need a hand?'

'This doesn't exactly feel like keeping it strictly business.' Col tilted his head.

She didn't like not being able to see his eyes; they always told her exactly how he was feeling. For a guy who'd been through what he had, he was still an open book. Anger, sadness and just about any other emotion showed itself so clearly on his face that he might as well have been a dictionary for feelings...at least where she was concerned.

She'd always liked that about him, envied it even. Elise had been raised to repress any extreme emotions. There were to be no tears, no screaming, no arguments in the Johnson household. Even hugs came at a premium. She'd never doubted that her parents loved her, but they were both hardened by their jobs in the police force and that hardness had infiltrated their home.

Falling apart in Col's arms that night had been the closest she'd ever come to true, unadulterated emotion. To honest emotion. And look where it had landed her.

'Besides, I thought you didn't want to talk about the past,' he said.

'We don't have to talk about it.' She sighed, unable to articulate why she wasn't yet ready to let him go. 'I thought you might need a hand with packing up his things and clearing out the rubbish.'

'I would be grateful for a hand.' He smiled, his lips pulling back to reveal an utterly disarming grin.

She nodded, warmth blossoming in her chest…and she was sure it wasn't from the sunshine. *You're walking on dangerous ground, Johnson. Very. Dangerous. Ground.*

Col's father's house was just as she remembered it from the few times she'd been there growing up. He'd never liked her visiting when he still lived at home and she had always suspected he was embarrassed by the strange stale alcohol smell and chaotic mess.

The garden was non-existent; the grass was brown in patches and completely absent in others. A few flowers within the clutches of death dotted the side fence and weeds sprouted up through the cracks in the cement path to the front door. The letterbox had taken a beating at some point, and the paint had chipped off in huge flakes. One of the numbers dangled from a single screw.

'Home sweet home,' Col said drily as they walked up to the front door.

What must he be feeling? Being forced to come home and deal with the house he'd fled as soon as he'd been able must be tough. Elise bit down on her lip as she followed him up the steps. At least he'd been able to escape the terrors of his childhood, she supposed. With this perspective she felt some of the anger at his departure slip away. Didn't everyone deserve the right to escape?

They walked through the front door and Elise wrinkled her nose at the smell. The stench of stale whisky hung in the air, mingling with cigarette smoke that seemed to have permeated the house's furnishings and walls. A cardboard box overflowed with empty bottles of whisky, bourbon and beer. The room itself held little more than a couch—which had seen better days—and a coffee table strewn with newspapers, betting stubs and ash from an overflowing ashtray.

'It looks…exactly as I remember it.' Elise wandered around, careful not to trip on the numerous clusters of mess around the floor, a deep ache settling in her chest. This was no place for a child to have grown up.

'Apparently my father didn't feel the need to clean,' Col replied, anger heavy in his voice. 'Or adhere to basic hygiene. Old habits die hard, I guess.'

'I guess,' she echoed, turning to Col in time to see the mask of his composure slip for a second.

White-hot rage flashed through his features as he zeroed in on a photo frame on the mantel. He strode across the room and picked it up. The photo had yellowed with time, the colours not as vibrant as they once had been. But it was undoubtedly Col and his father. A gap-toothed smile stared back, but the faint outline of a bruise marred the young boy's upper arm.

'He made me smile for this photo.' Col's voice shook, his shoulders bunched around his neck, jaw clenched. 'He shook me until I agreed to smile. And now he has this photo up like it's a goddamn happy memory.'

Her chest compressed. She wanted to reach and touch him; she wanted to ease his pain. But she didn't know what to do. She was so emotionally inept herself that she had no idea how to deal with this extreme emotion. Shame washed over her but she knew it wouldn't even show a glimmer on her face.

'Col—'

'I thought I was over this. I thought I was over *him*.'

The last word came out as a growl as he hurled the photo against a wall.

The glass exploded in a shower of tinkling particles. Elise watched them fall to the floor as if in slow motion, the sound of her heart magnified in her ears.

'I'm sorry, Elise. You shouldn't have had to see that.' He turned his pain, palpable in the air around him, inwards. His chest rose and fell too quickly as he clutched at self-control.

'It's okay.' She was frozen, rooted to the spot.

'I shouldn't have brought you here. I know you don't want to talk about the past—'

She couldn't comfort him with words, but she needed to ease his pain. So she did the only thing that she could do, the only thing that felt natural.

Her hands found Col's neck and she dragged him down to her, her open mouth ready for his. Their tongues met with force, lips pressing hard. This wasn't a comforting kiss. Hell, it wasn't even a distracting kiss. It was a full-on, all-barriers-down, forget-everything-else kiss.

One strong arm wrapped around her waist and lifted her so she could wind her legs around his waist. He moved and her back hit the wall, knocking the wind out of her. Col's teeth came down on her lip, his hips grinding into her open legs.

'My God, Elise,' he groaned against her hair as her lips found the lobe of his ear.

He had her pinned and she couldn't have found anything sexier at that point. The hard length of him had all her senses firing at high speed, his hands cupping her arse to hold her in place.

She writhed against him, eliciting a guttural moan

from the back of his throat. Up close his scent invaded her, making her dizzy with lust and memories. His short hair was silky against her palms; she gripped it and tugged his head down. His tongue flicked against hers, his faint minty taste drawing her in to keep the kiss going on and on.

'I've missed you,' he breathed.

The air was sucked out of her, reality crashing down like a derelict building—ugly and grey and harsh. 'No.'

'No?' He pulled his mouth away from hers, his dark brows crinkled above his nose.

She pushed against his chest until he released her, her sneakers hitting the ground with a thud. 'You don't get to say that to me.'

'What?'

'That you missed me.' She was breathing as heavily as if she'd run a marathon, her chest rising and falling rapidly. 'You *don't* get to talk to me like you wanted it any other way.'

'Damn, Elise.' He shook his head, rubbing the back of his neck with one hand. '*You* kissed me.'

'I didn't know what else to do.' She glared at him, the old feelings of anger and shame returning with force. The feelings roared within her, crashing into one another and fighting for her attention, but she swallowed them down.

'And kissing is your go-to move?' he cried. 'How am I supposed to respond to that?'

'Oh, so you only kissed me because I kissed you first?' Her chest burned, the heat clawing at her neck and face.

'That's *not* what I said.'

'What are you trying to say, then, Col? You're not

being very articulate.' She looked around for her hand-bag. 'Or is that because all your blood has rushed away from your brain?'

'That's a cheap shot.'

'If the shoe fits.'

He looked exasperated. 'That doesn't even make sense.'

'Forget it ever happened, Col. A momentary slip.' She found her bag on the floor next to the couch. 'It won't happen again.'

'Ellie, wait.' He reached out to her.

'Forget it. We should have kept this to business like we agreed.' She strode to the door, his footsteps close on her heels.

'Then why did you kiss me?' He spun her around so that she was sandwiched between the front door and the expanse of his chest.

Why *did* she do it? Because after all he'd done she still wanted him as badly as she did before? Because he was the only guy who'd ever been able to get close without spooking her? She'd had two short-term relationships since he'd left and both of them ended the same way: swiftly and without the opportunity for reconciliation. The last guy had left her with a parting shot that stung for weeks and weeks. He'd called her an emotionally devoid robot. The other had said he couldn't be with someone who was so distant all the time, who couldn't talk about how she felt, express what she wanted.

'Why, Ellie?' he pressed. 'Answer me.'

She couldn't do it; her throat closed around the words and stifled them until they disappeared. Her mouth opened and closed, almost involuntarily. She felt herself shut down; it always happened when she was trapped.

There was no way for her to express herself that she knew. She couldn't cry; she couldn't be honest. So she simply closed up shop and berated herself on the inside.

'I see.' He nodded, stepping aside to give her space to leave.

She bit down on her lip so hard the metallic twang of blood seeped onto her tongue. What would a normal person do? They would scream, they would let the feelings out, they would at least say something…but her tongue was a dead weight in her mouth.

He stayed silent as she opened the door and slipped out, shame compressing her chest. For the first time since he left, Elise understood why Col had left her.

CHAPTER SIX

As the sound of her footsteps faded into nothingness Col let out every expletive he knew. He should have guessed her kiss was too good to be true. How could he have let himself slip like that?

He shook his head, leaning back against the door to survey the house and clear his head. Why did he want so desperately to hear the words from her lips? It was exactly the reason he'd called up the PR and Communications Manager at Google to change his mind and say he would come to Australia after all. No, he wasn't going to do this now. He had a house to clean and business to take care of.

Soon he'd be back in the US and in the comfort of his own home, his own office. An empty ache opened up in the pit of his stomach…but what then? He'd known before he came back to Australia that his life had stalled. He was frequently frustrated, lonely…isolated. The only family he'd ever known was Elise, Rich and their parents. He had no one else, apart from his PR manager, Pete, who wanted him for something other than his fortune. Even Pete was still on his payroll. Elise was different.

But he had to face facts. Elise didn't want him at

all. That was clear from the fact that she could turn her passion on and off like a switch…that wasn't true feeling. That was a game, but he wanted so much more and nothing would change that.

After Col had filled six garbage bags to the brim and taken them all out to the Dumpster outside, he stood on the front steps looking out into the street. The neighbourhood hadn't changed much over the years; it was still quiet and while it wasn't exactly the home of the white-picket-fence dream it *was* simple and tidy. Unsurprisingly, his father's house was still the eyesore of the whole street.

Col's phone vibrated, bringing his attention back to the present. 'Hello?'

'Hey, man.' The voice of his friend and head of PR for Hillam Technologies came down the line.

'Pete.' Col grinned. The heavy New York accent always put a smile on his face. 'Have you landed?'

'I landed this morning, but it was stupid early.' Pete yawned. 'I'm thinking it's beer o'clock by now. We should meet so I can go over the conference schedule with you.'

'I'll meet you at the hotel.'

Half an hour later Col and Pete were seated at an open-air bar close to the hotel, two pints of pale ale and a full itinerary for the conference in front of them. Though Pete might have looked like the kind of guy who lived a laid-back lifestyle—with his overlong blond hair and lazy smile—he ran Col's public relations department with the kind of militant attention to detail better suited to an intelligence operative.

The itinerary was highlighted and labelled with colour-coded tabs. Pete's precise handwriting added extra notes and instructions.

Col took a swig of his beer. 'It looks like you're planning to break into Fort Knox.'

'You don't pay me to wing it.' Pete's eyes wandered as a waitress in a pair of tiny shorts walked past. 'And this conference is a big deal. The kind of exposure we're going to get is massive. This could be what helps us break into Asia.'

Pete's eyes glittered and Col thought to himself, for what must have been the hundredth time over the last five years, that he was glad to have met him. Hiring him was an even better decision.

With the way he'd left things in Australia, Col's friendship with Rich hadn't exactly been in the best condition. As the years had crawled by they'd spoken less and less, and Col couldn't even ask after Elise without her brother making a snide remark about broken promises. Pete had been Col's first friend in America; he was the wacky guy who lived in the apartment next door and who was always spouting grand plans and ideas for business world domination.

Turned out, some of those ideas were actually pretty lucrative. When Col's previous PR manager had left to join Google he'd hired Pete and never once regretted it.

'I can feel in my gut, man.' Pete slapped his palm against the table, causing some of his beer to slosh over the edge of the glass. 'Your keynote speech is going to set the tone for next year. I can see TED talk invitations, LinkedIn will be after you for their influencer program…'

'Let's take it one step at a time.'

Close as they might be, Pete was unaware of Col's

issues with public speaking. He had assumed that, like many technologists, Col was a bit on the introverted side. But the two men often battled about whether or not Col should get more active in the media, and Pete was dogged in his attempt to turn Col and Hillam Technologies into *the* IT company of the social-media generation. Unfortunately for Col, that meant constant requests for him to appear in the public eye as not only the face of the company but as an industry personality.

'How's everything going with your dad's stuff?'

The sudden change of topic caught Col off guard and he clutched his beer for a moment while he thought how to answer the question.

'It's…' he sighed '…getting there.'

Pete chuckled. 'That was a non-committal statement if I ever heard one. Don't tell me your reluctance to talk has something to do with a certain female.'

'A certain female?' Col zeroed in on his friend. He'd never mentioned Elise before, at least not to anyone he worked with.

'An ex-ballerina, perhaps?'

'How do you know about that?' He took another swig on his beer, wondering why his life was of so much interest to others. Couldn't they just leave him alone to do his own thing?

'That darling assistant of yours mentioned something about having to get all PI and find a phone number for you. She stumbled across a bunch of photos of this very good-looking ballerina.' Pete grinned. 'So who is she?'

'Dammit, Chelsea,' Col cursed under his breath. His assistant should know better than to divulge information to anyone.

'Don't blame her. I happened to walk past her desk

when the photos were up and, well…' He chuckled. 'You know she's susceptible to my charms.'

'You're full of it.'

'I'm not letting you change the topic.' Pete signalled for the waitress to bring them another couple of beers but Col changed his to a soda water.

'Why is my love life of such interest anyway?'

'Who said anything about a love life?'

Col sighed. 'She's an old friend. I wanted to see her while I was here. That's it.'

'If that's it then why are you getting your panties in a twist?' Pete narrowed his light eyes and studied him. 'You slept with her, didn't you?'

'Not this time,' Col grumbled.

'Oh, come on! You can't clam up now. I'm living vicariously, man.'

Pete was halfway through a bet with his brother that he could go without sex for a whole year. There was a vintage E-type Jaguar up for grabs and Pete was, as always, determined to win.

'It's been six months, come on. Tell me at least one of us is getting laid.'

Col sighed. 'I'm afraid not, my friend. That ship has sailed.'

'Why? I don't believe for a second that you lost interest. Ballerinas are smoking hot.' Pete waggled his brows. 'And bendy.'

'Interest wasn't lacking, that's for sure. Unfortunately there was a whole lot of baggage. I was best friends with her brother and he wasn't exactly cool with us being together.'

'Oh.' Pete nodded sagely. 'Older brother?'

'Yeah. Protective as all hell. It was pretty much the reason I left Australia.'

'And now?'

'Now.' Col sighed. 'It's still as damn complicated as it ever was.'

'But she's worth it, right?'

Unfortunately Col's head and heart couldn't quite agree on the answer to that. Gut feeling said he would never find another girl who made him feel the way Elise did, but his head always pointed out the obvious fact. Even if he did accept his feelings for Elise, could she return them?

The next evening Col found himself unable to unwind. He'd spent the day signing documentation for the estate, going over the details for his father's funeral and working through some last-minute details for the Hillam Technologies conference stand with Pete. Now his head was filled with too much information, too much emotion and a healthy dose of sexual frustration, thanks to the memory of his kiss with Elise.

It was Friday night and the city was ablaze with people enjoying the hot summer's evening. Col had gone out to get some air but the area surrounding his hotel was densely packed and noisy. He was restless, it wasn't yet late enough to call his office and deal with work problems but he had nothing else to do. Practising his speech had turned him into a bundle of agitated energy and he had the feeling it would only make matters worse if he kept at it.

He played with his phone, turning it over in his hand. He was about to tap his pin to unlock the screen when Elise's face flashed up.

'Ellie?'

'Hey, Col.' She sounded nervous; he could hear the slight lift in her pitch as she said his name. 'Look, I wanted to say sorry about yesterday. I…'

There was a pause on the other end of the line. Her breathing came in unsteady little puffs.

'I know I went from hot to cold and I flipped out. I was the one who started the kiss and I…' She sighed. 'I didn't know what to do.'

He swallowed. This might just constitute the first apology he'd ever received from Elise. Perhaps he was wrong…perhaps she *had* changed. That thought was a confusing can of worms, because if she had indeed changed then things might have been different between them.

But he couldn't deal with that right now. 'It's fine.'

'Look, I have another performance-related activity for you…if you're up to it?'

'I guess that depends on what it is.' He frowned. 'This better not include any toddlers.'

'No toddlers,' she said with a laugh. 'The dance company that Jasmine is with has rehearsals tonight. They often have family and friends watch.'

Going to the ballet felt like a stretch. 'And that will help me how?'

'When they practise they make mistakes. I want you to see that the world won't fall apart if you make a mistake while someone is watching.'

Hadn't that been the exact reason he'd hidden away his whole life, carrying with him that dislike of being in the spotlight well into adulthood, driving Pete crazy with his constant questioning of why he needed to be at certain events? It wasn't as if he were the recluse people said he was, he was just…private. The less attention he drew to himself, the better.

'It'll be good for you, Col. Plus, I'll shout you a drink afterwards…to make up for yesterday.'

'Where should I meet you?'

She gave him the address and he was grateful to escape the oppressive weekend crowd in the city. The drive was short but traffic was as thick and heavy as the summer air. He drummed his fingers against the steering wheel, tapping an erratic beat while he waited to approach the turn-off to the rehearsal venue.

After he parked his car he sat for a moment, contemplating how to deal with Elise and her hot-cold attitude. He raked a hand through his hair and got out of the car. He was a sucker for punishment where Elise Johnson was concerned, and that hadn't changed a damn iota in five years.

The theatre was old, a heritage-listed building, with ornate plasterwork and faded red and gold carpet all the way through. It was the perfect contrast to the ultramodern, bordering-on-strange music that floated up to the high ceiling. A group of dancers stretched out on stage, Jasmine amongst them.

Elise was sitting in the front row; he recognised the back of her blonde head instantly with all its wispy hairs escaping into a soft gold halo. She turned, waving and motioning for him to join her. He wasn't sure how this was supposed to help—dancers on a stage felt so far removed from his situation. How would his mind make the connection? Was there a chance she asked him here just to spend time with him?

'Hey.' Her face tilted up to his as he came closer; she bit down on her lower lip and patted the seat next to her.

'Hey.'

He lowered himself next to her, totally aware of the closeness of their thighs, their shoulders. If they turned to face one another they would be a hair's breadth away from kissing. Heat crawled through him, making his limbs heavy with wanting. As much as he knew he should stop thinking about their kiss the day before, he couldn't. As soon as he'd lowered his head to hers the old desire had come flooding back, brighter and more intense than at any point in the last five years. It was a lesson he couldn't learn, a memory he couldn't forget, a desire he couldn't deny.

The dancers set up on stage, the choreographer standing with his back to the small and scattered audience. He barked orders in a thick German accent and the dancers assembled; slow and haunting music filled the room punctuated by violin and a heavy beat.

He watched Elise from the corner of his eye. She sat, enraptured. Her hands gripped her knees, white-knuckled. Her beautiful twilight eyes were wide, shimmering.

The spell was broken when one of the dancers stumbled out of a lift, falling backwards and bumping into another pair with a loud '*ooof*'. Col scanned the audience. No one appeared to be laughing, pointing, smirking. They simply waited while the dancers reassembled themselves and started over.

'Jasmine looks like she's doing well,' Col said, turning to Elise.

He'd known the serious brunette nearly as long as he'd known Elise. Those two had been inseparable growing up…except for the times that he and Elise had stolen a secret moment away when her brother wasn't watching.

A sad smile passed across her lips. 'She's made a lot of changes in the last few months. She met someone a while ago and he's done her a world of good.'

Jasmine's willowy frame stretched out on stage, her long limbs forming beautiful and unusual shapes, but Col couldn't pay attention. His eyes kept drifting to Elise and the way she bounced her knee rapidly as she watched the stage, her lips pulled into a line.

'Do you miss it?'

'What?' she asked, turning back to him. 'Dancing?'

'Yeah.'

'Sometimes.' She shrugged. 'But then sometimes I don't.'

Typical Elise answer: non-committal…closed off. He sighed and nodded, turning back to the stage.

'I can't miss something that was never going anywhere.' She said it so quietly that he might easily have missed it.

'What do you mean?'

She opened her mouth to speak but the choreographer turned around and shushed them. Her face closed off, the walls shooting up around her as the moment disintegrated before his eyes. She smiled brightly at him and pointed to the stage, turning so that he could only see her perfect, pert-nosed profile.

The combination of sitting so close to Col and seeing her best friend dance with an abandon she herself could never achieve was doing funny things to her insides. Her heart fluttered unsteadily, its uneven rhythm making her restless. Elise kept her hands braced on her knees to keep from reaching out to touch him, training her eyes firmly on the scene in front of them.

Jasmine moved with a passion and emotion that stirred a small inkling of jealousy deep within her chest. How different her life might've been if she could let her barriers down: perhaps her career wouldn't have stalled; perhaps she could have done more to help her mother; perhaps Col might have stayed. An uncomfortable lump filled the pit of her stomach and she pressed a hand against it to quell the rocking sensation.

The rehearsal concluded without another word passing between Col and Elise. He sat beside her, tense as she was, hands knotted in his lap and brows furrowed. If there was ever a moment that they could have reconciled the past, yesterday had been it. He'd tried to tell her how he felt, tried to tell her *exactly* what she'd wanted to hear...but she hadn't listened. She'd pushed him away because it was the only way to deal with the emotions coursing through her.

The dancers left the stage, gathering their things and exiting the old theatre in dribs and drabs.

'I've cleared it with the dance company so we can have a look around,' Elise said, pushing up from her seat.

Col folded his arms across his chest, his shadow dwarfing her. 'Are you going to try to make me practise again?'

'Try? There is no try. I'm in charge of this partnership, remember.'

'You'd like to think that.' He let out a sharp laugh, taunting her, challenging her. 'Wouldn't you?'

'Come on, less arguing, more exploring.' She darted up the stairs at the side of the stage and stood in the middle, looking out into the audience.

Most of the dancers had cleared out. Only Jasmine

hovered in the front row pretending to check through her exercise bag, but Elise knew she was keeping an eye on her. The stage was smooth beneath her sneakers, the wooden surface worn down under many feet over many years. A few steps and then she'd stop. Okay, maybe a *pirouette* or two.

Col had followed her up onto the stage and he stood at the edge, thick arms folded across his broad chest. She kept her eyes on him as she danced, a strange sensation fizzing inside her. An *arabesque* turned into a *fondu* followed by a few quick steps; she turned and floated her arms above her head. She felt the hem of her silky top rise up; cool air brushed the exposed sliver of belly.

Heat coursed through her. She'd never ever felt like this when dancing before. Perhaps this was the feeling her teachers had tried to elicit from her when they'd chanted at her over and over: *show me the passion, show me what you feel, just show...something.* She stopped, suddenly noticing the way Col was looking at her, hungry and tortured and barely restrained.

'You've still got the moves,' he said, stalking up to her in his usual purposeful stride. 'Not that I had any doubt you'd ever lose them.'

'Thanks for the vote of confidence.' She gave a little shimmy and laughed, drunk on the feeling of his appreciative gaze on her. Her heart kicked up a notch, molten heat seeping down to her stomach.

'Why did you stop dancing anyway? You were pretty good from memory.'

Pretty good was an understatement. She'd trained since she was old enough to stand up on her own and she'd landed herself a role in the Australian Ballet's *corps de ballet.* She was more than 'pretty good'. Unfortunately the technique that she studied with obsession had also been her downfall.

'I stalled.' She looked away, leaving the memory hanging thick in the air.

'Stalled?'

'My dancing was too…safe.' *Just like the rest of my life.*

The sound of a throat clearing broke the spell, and their heads snapped to the front of the stage. Jasmine picked up her bag and looked pointedly at Elise. 'Are you coming?'

She hesitated. 'I'm sure Col can give me a lift.'

'I'll make sure she gets home safe,' he replied, the deep timbre of his voice sending a shiver down her spine.

'Are you sure?' Jasmine narrowed her eyes at Elise as if trying to talk to her telepathically. Elise had a good idea of what she might be saying: *wrong way, turn back before it's too late.*

'I'm sure.'

She could feel the space between her and Col, every millimetre crackling and sparking with energy. 'Let's have a look out the back.'

They walked through the wings and entered the small backstage area, which was cluttered with props and costumes. A long velvet cloak hung from a hook; the white fur trimming the hood had gone grey with age. A light film of dust coated the furniture. It looked as though it could have been a room in a funfair's haunted house.

'Why are we really here, Elise?' Col stood close behind her; his frame seemed even bigger in the cramped space.

The scent of his cinnamon aftershave mingled with the charming, old-theatre smell of talcum powder and faded dreams. His breath came hot against her neck. He didn't touch her and yet she could feel his intentions as heavily as if he'd laid both hands on her. He wanted her, like that one night all those years ago; she felt his desire so keenly because it matched her own.

She swallowed, willing her voice to hold steady. 'I'm helping you prepare for your keynote speech.'

'Bullshit.' Hot breath, so close…so very close.

The backstage area was dimly lit, bright light only filtering in from the stage itself. Golden beams were filled with dancing dust motes, the hazy light making the dark spaces seem even more blackened and mysterious.

'If you don't want my help then we should leave.' She turned; her nose met with the hard wall of his chest. 'Now.'

'I want you to tell me why you called me here.'

'I told you already.' A lump lodged in her throat. Was she so transparent? Could he see right through her?

'You gave me the reason you use to lie to yourself.'

'I'm not lying.' She stepped back, desperate for space between them and yet hating it at the same time.

'Are you being totally honest?'

She wanted to say yes, but then she'd be lying, wouldn't she? Why couldn't she tell him how she felt, how much his leaving had hurt her, how much she wanted with all her heart to forgive him and hold him and never let him go? But the words stuck in her throat, threatening to choke her. She was a failure at relationships; she was a failure at love and emotion and honesty.

'Can I plead the fifth?'

'Not in Australia.' He sighed, rubbing a hand down his jaw.

The shadows in the backstage area made his stubble seem heavier, made the angle of his jaw seem sharper, the slash of his cheekbones harsher. Only the dazzling white of his teeth and the faded blue of his eyes broke the darkness.

'What do you want from me, Col?' She threw her hands up in the air, more frustrated by her own lack of control than by his probing questions.

'How about a little honesty?' He cocked his head, stepping closer again so that he was almost upon her. 'I want to know what's going on inside that pretty head of yours.'

She took another step back. 'I can't give you that.'

'You can't tell me what you're thinking?' He advanced again, forcing her back until she bumped into a pile of crates.

He flattened his palm against the crate and she had the irresistible urge to turn her face and kiss the smooth, perfect skin on the inside of his wrist. She wanted to run her tongue along the vein that created a subtle ridge up his arm; she wanted to nip at the tender flesh on the inside of his elbow. Ugh, she was like a hormonal, sex-starved teenager!

'No.' Her voice shook and she hated herself for it.

His pupils flared until she felt as if she were looking into two bottomless pits. 'Are you sure?'

'I can't tell you about things I shouldn't be thinking.'

He stood in front of her, unblinking and frozen. Memories struck with a force that almost pulled her feet out from under her. *I can't tell you about things I shouldn't be thinking...* She'd said those exact words to

him five years ago, the night before he left, the night before *everything* fell apart. He'd come to her; he'd asked
her what their night together meant.

She'd been young, inexperienced, emotionally underdeveloped. She'd shrugged her shoulders and made
light of them sleeping together, assuming that he was
looking for an out. When she'd laughed his questions
off, the hurt in his eyes had been a stake through her
heart. Yet here she was again, same words, still pushing him away. She wanted to blame him for leaving,
but deep down she knew that half the blame rested on
her shoulders.

'Why shouldn't you be thinking about these things?'

'Because…' She drew a breath. 'Because, we're like
family. We should have left it that way.'

Her brother would have been furious if he'd known
about them. He'd made her promise as a teenager that
she'd never kiss Col…and she assumed that promise
extended to things much more grown up than kissing.
Rich had made her swear on their parents' lives and
the very day after she broke that promise her dad died.
She'd never told Col that.

Elise closed her eyes, her head swimming with the
weight of the past. Adult sensibilities told her that sleeping with Col hadn't caused her father to die. But the
child within said that if she'd kept her promise to Rich
then maybe everything would have been…different.

'You're right.' Col stepped back. 'We shouldn't have
crossed that line. I never wanted to leave you, Ellie. I
was young, confused—'

'Stop it.' Her breath came in heavy mouthfuls, ragged
and painful. 'I don't want to talk about this anymore.'

'Fine.' His face was a mask of composure, his light eyes cold and still as a frozen lake. 'I'll take you home.'

'Col—'

'You said you didn't want to talk anymore, so don't do it for my benefit.'

Her heart felt as though it were splintering all over again, but as they walked past an old mirror the face that reflected back was totally devoid of feeling. She was doing the right thing; she could never give Col what he needed. Even if she could muster up the guts to try it would only end in tears...and they wouldn't be hers.

CHAPTER SEVEN

ELISE LEANT BACK in her chair behind the reception desk of the EJ Ballet School, tilting her face up to the steady stream of cold air blowing from the air conditioner. For the first time in weeks the studio's waiting area didn't feel like a greenhouse thanks to the portly man in overalls who'd just left. The first half of Col's payment had arrived that day and she'd immediately called her maintenance guy.

'Hey, it's fixed!' Jasmine said as she and Missy exited the studio.

They had been practising a routine together, and were due to perform at a fund-raising concert in a few weeks' time. Both girls were glowing with perspiration as they jostled for the main spot in front of the air conditioner.

'Thanks for getting this fixed, Ellie. This is officially the best place in Melbourne right now.' Missy swept back a few stray strands of her vibrant copper hair and sighed happily.

'So, uh…how were you able to get it fixed?' Jasmine turned to her, her dark eyes narrowed suspiciously.

Elise could feel the lecture coming on, and after what happened with Col last night she didn't want to talk about it. So she pretended not to hear as she flipped through a copy of *Pointe* magazine, holding it high enough up that she blocked out Jasmine's motherly stare.

A hand came over the top of her magazine and slowly lowered it so that she was looking straight at Jasmine. 'You accepted his offer, didn't you?'

'What's going on?' Missy left the comfort of the air-conditioning unit to join them at the reception desk.

'I did what I had to do,' Elise said, snatching her magazine back and laying it in her in-tray. 'I'm saving my business.'

'By getting mixed up with the guy who bailed on you as soon as things got tough, *after* your family took him in and cared for him?' She huffed, crossing her slim arms across her chest. 'Doesn't sound like someone who's very trustworthy to me.'

Jasmine's distrust of Col wasn't exactly based on fact, rather an assumption that Elise had never bothered to correct. Her friend had *assumed* that Col left the country after her father's death, knowing the truth. In Jasmine's eyes Col was a deserter.

'There's more to it than that.' Elise shook her head, the blood pounding in her temples. She wasn't ready to deal with this yet, but she felt a sudden urge to correct Jasmine's assumptions. 'There's more to *him* than that.'

'Yeah, right.' Jasmine rolled her eyes. 'I'm worried about you, Ellie. You've always had a thing for him and he's…bad news.'

'Are you talking about Col?' Missy asked.

Elise nodded. Jasmine and Missy had been regulars at the Johnson family table; the three of them had driven the rest of Elise's family mad by practising their routines in the lounge room while *Wheel of Fortune* was on.

'The boy whose father was a drunk, who hit him.' Jasmine's eyes were wide as she reached out and grabbed Elise's hand. 'Don't you remember that he used to turn up at the house and scream at your parents? He would bang on the door until your dad threatened to take him down to the police station. God, could you imagine what would have happened if your parents weren't both cops?'

'That was Col's father, *not* Col. He's nothing like that.'

'I'm not saying he's the same, but I don't want you getting mixed up with his family. I want you to be safe.'

Elise sighed. 'He's dead, Jas. Col's father is dead. That's why he's in the country.'

Col had never explicitly asked her not to say anything, but she imagined he wanted to keep it quiet. Wasn't that why he'd changed his name from Colby Hill to Colby Hillam? He wanted to keep his past locked away on the other side of the world. She needed to figure out whether he considered her part of the shameful past or not.

'Didn't I encourage you to take a chance on Grant?' Elise swung her legs down from the front desk and climbed out of her chair, relishing the cold stream of air blowing against her heated cheeks and neck.

'If my memory serves me correctly you used some good old-fashioned reverse psychology.' Jasmine raked a hand through her long dark hair, a begrudging smile on her lips.

'Potato, pot-*ah*-to. It got the right result, didn't it?'

'I say you should go for it,' said Missy, folding her

arms across her chest when she received a glare from Jasmine. 'What?'

'I'm trying to get you the right result. I'm worried about you, Ellie.' Jasmine reached out and touched her shoulder. 'I don't want to see you make the same mistake twice.'

'What if it's not a mistake this time?' That was a confusing thought. Why was it so much easier when Col was a whole continent away? 'Col didn't know about Dad when he left. He's not the person you think he is.'

Jasmine raised a perfectly arched brow, her mouth forming a small 'o'. 'He didn't know?'

Elise shook her head. 'He checked in as soon as he found out. But Rich told him not to come back. He told Col that everything was okay…that we didn't need him here.'

'Oh.' Realisation dawned in Jasmine's eyes, the defensiveness seeping from her posture. 'Why didn't you tell me any of this?'

'I was angry.' Elise grabbed her bag and moved towards the door. 'Now, I don't want to talk about this any more.'

'You *have* to talk about things, Ellie. Didn't we agree that you wouldn't shut us out again?' Missy tugged at a spiral of copper-coloured hair as she implored her with turquoise eyes.

'I'm not shutting you out, girls.' Elise put her hands up as if to surrender. 'I just need to think about this, and it's a little hard to work through things with good angel and bad angel interrupting my thoughts.'

'I'm good angel, right?' Missy asked, elbowing Jasmine in the ribs.

'No, you're the *bad* angel.' Jasmine pursed her lips, ever the serious mother hen of their little group.

'I'll be fine.' Elise dodged a group of young students filtering in for their class. 'And I'm not shutting you out. I promise.'

Outside the sun was setting and the air was thick; the summer was resisting coming to a close. She fanned herself as she walked to her car, slipping inside and rolling down the windows to let some of the heat out.

Col's handsome face danced in front of her eyes. She'd come so close to kissing him again last night, she wasn't sure how much longer she would be able to resist. The main question was, would she regret it more if she let him go without tasting him again or if she gave in and lost him a second time? The conference was tomorrow and his father's funeral must be soon after. Then he'd be gone...again.

The conference. Guilt swished in her stomach. He'd hired her to help him prepare for his speech and what had she done? Other than humiliate him in front of a group of toddlers and take him to a dance rehearsal just because she wanted to see him...yet she'd taken his money.

A lump lodged in her throat. It was wrong; taking his money for doing so little went against everything she believed in. Yes, she'd been desperately trying to avoid the confrontation of letting one of her teachers go and not dealing with the real reasons why her life was a massive failure.

She had to give the money back...well, minus what she paid the air-con guy, but perhaps he would consider that little bit to be a loan. Then she could get back on her feet and repay him later. She couldn't wait. She needed to see him now; she needed to tell him that she planned to return the money. At least that way when he left, she wouldn't have the burden of being indebted to him.

At last the clean-up of his father's place was complete. There had been a supremely awkward encounter with his father's girlfriend who wanted to stake claim on a few items of furniture and a framed picture of them both. Col had never met her before, but her sad eyes and quivering lip told him that at least one person was mourning the death of the late Arthur Hill.

He wondered if the girlfriend knew about Arthur's shady past and his abusive tendencies... He hoped for her sake that Arthur had at least given up his temper if not his addiction to alcohol. Though he seriously doubted it.

All that remained of the estate had been collected by a charity, with the exception of the items he gave to the girlfriend. She'd tried to convince him to keep the photograph he'd thrown at the wall a few days ago, but he crumpled the old paper in his palm. There was no way he wanted to keep a single thing from his childhood; the internal scarring was enough.

Now he wanted a shower—perhaps the rush of hot water would clear his mind. He needed to get last night's encounter with Elise out of his head and focus on preparing for the conference tomorrow. So much to do, so little headspace with which to deal with it all.

He stripped, showered until his fingertips shrivelled and strode out into the main room with a towel around his waist. Daylight was fading, the last red-gold beams of sunlight dipping in the distance. The city had turned on its lights, glittering bulbs scattered across the view like sand on a breeze.

A knock at the door broke him out of his reverie. He frowned. Usually room service announced itself but no voice followed the knock.

'Who is it?' He approached the door, wary. If this was another reporter trying to catch him off guard…

'It's me. Elise.'

He pulled the door open and stifled an amused smile as a shocked 'O' formed on her utterly delectable lips. Her eyes traversed his naked torso and it was all Col could do to restrain himself from puffing out his chest under her appreciative gaze.

'Did you come for any reason in particular or was it just so you could admire the view?' he asked.

She recovered quickly, her blonde brows narrowing as she shoved her upturned nose in the air. 'I came to talk. If I only wanted abs I wouldn't have bothered to trek into the city, I can get that off the internet.'

'Well, since you're not here to indulge your internet porn fantasies in person…' he stepped back and opened the door wider '…do come in.'

He didn't miss the flush that peeked out from the modest neckline of her grey top. The colour matched her eyes perfectly, and the long chain that hung down past her breast was weighted with a horseshoe. She fiddled with it as she stood in the middle of the room, rolling her eyes at him.

'Have I ever told you just how full of it you are?'

'Frequently.'

'So long as we're on the same page.' She smirked.

'How did you find me? I don't think I told you where I was staying and I never got a call from Reception.'

'The same way you got my number when you arrived here without warning.' She folded her arms across her chest, forcing the small curve of her breasts upwards.

'You called my assistant?'

'I did some sleuthing,' she corrected.

'Are we suddenly in a Nancy Drew novel?' He laughed, feeling some of the tension release from behind his eyes. Elise had always had that effect on him. 'Is this Elise Johnson and the case of the missing CEO?'

'I'll turn it into a murder mystery if you're not careful.' Her lip twitched. 'I know this is your favourite hotel—you told me so once when I did a performance here. I figured you'd have the penthouse suite, so I came up.'

'How did you get up without a swipe card?'

'I told the cleaning lady I was your sister.'

'And she fell for that?'

'I'm very convincing.' She grinned, and he didn't doubt for a second that she could charm the pants off anyone she set her sights on. It'd certainly worked on him.

'I'm flattered that you went to such lengths to come and see me, though you could have just called.' He folded his arms across his chest, wondering for a second if he'd knotted his towel tight enough. 'Why are you here?'

'Not to see you naked, if that's what you're thinking.'

'I wasn't.' Okay, so maybe he was.

She took a deep breath and unfolded her arms as if making a conscious decision not to block him out. 'I came to tell you that I'm returning your money.'

'You're what?'

His chest constricted. Was this her way of telling

him that she wanted to sever all ties? He knew that his trip to Australia would be short-lived, but with each passing day there was a niggling sensation that perhaps things could be different between them. The fact that he thought that after their last few encounters was saying something.

'I don't feel right taking this money. The only reason I did it was because I was desperate to save my studio.' She blew out a long breath, and shifted her weight. Her fingers toyed with the gold horseshoe. 'But it was the wrong thing to do. I got myself into this mess and I need to get myself out. I shouldn't be taking charity from you—'

'It's *not* charity.'

'Yes, it is. I haven't really helped you at all. Though I did tell you I was the wrong person…' She looked up at him, sucking on her bottom lip for a moment before continuing. 'It doesn't feel right, I shouldn't have taken money from you knowing I couldn't help.'

'God, Elise.' Col raked a hand through his wet hair, sending droplets of water over his neck and shoulders. 'I would have given you the money anyway.'

'So it *was* charity!'

'You're like family to me. Hell, you're the only family I've ever known and no matter what I do I just can't seem to get it right. It's not charity, it's one person trying to look after someone they care about.'

She folded her arms back across her chest and looked out of the window. There she went again, shutting down the second things got real. But he didn't want to stop, couldn't stop. Something deep in his gut compelled him to say the words that he'd held inside five years ago.

'You did everything for me growing up—your family did everything for me. And what did I have to give in return? A big, fat nothing.'

Years had passed but the shame hadn't lessened. Therapy had dulled his rage to a manageable roar, but it was still there quietly haunting him at every turn. He wasn't strong enough to stop his father, he wasn't strong enough to protect himself…at least he hadn't been. Now his sights were set firmly on a level of success so atmospheric that no one could possibly call him a loser again.

So what if he wanted to use some of that success to help Elise out? What was so bad about that? Deep down he'd known that she couldn't cure him of his public-speaking phobia. Hell, even the therapist hadn't been able to totally fix that one. But being around Elise calmed him, it always had…and that was an improvement he needed right now.

'I don't want your charity.' She didn't look at him.

Emotion welled up inside him and he knew he had to do something before he blurted out words that couldn't be taken back. He closed the space between them and grabbed her shoulders.

'Look at me,' he growled. 'I care about you, Elise. I care about you more than I've cared about anyone in my whole life. I never forgot about you, and believe me I tried.'

'Don't do this, Col.' She turned to him, grey eyes frosted over like ice on a windscreen—hard and opaque. 'I want to make things right.'

'And you think the way to make things right is by giving me my money back and pretending nothing ever happened between us?'

'Isn't it?' Not one of her muscles moved under his

hands. 'We're stuck in this weird, no-man's-land. We family, but we're not. We're lovers, but we're not.'

'We could be.' The words escaped his lips before he could even *think* about stopping them.

Why did he keep doing this? It was a situation that couldn't possibly work and yet she was a girl who deserved long-lasting, grow-old-together love. They'd known each other for over two decades and they still couldn't work one another out. It was doomed; *they* were doomed.

'I'm not like other girls, Col.' Her hands came up to his bare chest, the gentle press of her fingertips sending flames through him. 'I can't take something from you without giving something back. I don't want this to be what I give back. I want to give you something real.'

Her long, curling lashes fluttered and the ice started to melt. Her cheeks coloured, her breathing came faster and when she looked up at him he thought he might drown in the sincerity of her.

'I want to tell you something.' She swallowed. 'Something real.'

It was the best gift she could have given him, a glimpse of the truth that had been locked inside her head for so long that he'd thought he'd never be able to see behind her mask. His body swung the confusing distance between being incredibly turned on and totally sombre with the seriousness of what she was about to do. His body fired under her touch, every nerve-ending alight with the presence of her.

'I want to tell you why I quit ballet.'

Okay, so it wasn't quite what he was expecting but it was still a step in the right direction. He knew she'd quit her position with the Australian Ballet after her father died and assumed that was the reason.

'You know I studied very hard growing up,' she said, watching as he nodded. 'My aim was to be the best technical dancer the Australian Ballet had ever seen. I wanted to nail the angle of every *arabesque*. I wanted to perfect every turn, every lift. I wanted to be perfect. I was pretty damn close to being a "perfect" dancer. I never got a step wrong.'

'I'd call that perfect.'

'But I realised one day that in my quest to be the perfect dancer I'd missed a very important element. Emotion.'

Her chest rose and fell, her small breasts grazing against him ever so slightly. He bit down on his lip and willed himself not to get hard; he would not ruin this moment.

'I would watch other dancers like Missy and Jasmine and I could see this love, anguish and splendour pour out of them. Their faces would be like beacons. I even studied them so I could see if I could make my face do the same thing. But I realised then, as I was practising in front of a mirror, that I was forcing something which didn't exist.

'If I didn't *feel* the emotion, I couldn't fake it. There was something fundamentally missing and it meant I could never be as good as those other dancers. The teachers saw it—it's why I was never able to move out of the *corps de ballet*. They knew there was something missing that no amount of technique could make up for.'

His chest ached, not so much for the story itself but for the fact that even now she told it without an ounce of emotion in her voice. He knew it was there, unreachable beneath the surface of her carefully managed exterior. He wanted so desperately to kiss her, to kiss all of that pain away.

'The week before Dad died the director sat me down and told me that if I didn't find some way to bring out the emotion in my dancing then I wouldn't ever make it out of the *corps de ballet*. But I couldn't do it, I couldn't ever let go of the technique, the perfection. I couldn't *feel* the way other dancers feel. So, after Dad died, I decided that it wasn't worth continuing since I knew I'd never be able to get to the level I wanted.' She sighed. 'Sometimes I wonder if that was the right thing to do, but I'm glad I opened the ballet school. It brings me a lot of joy to see these young dancers find the pleasure that I missed out on.'

He had to keep himself in check; the protective urges that roared through him threatened to overtake his sensibilities. He wanted to bundle her up into his arms and never let her go. To some her story might have seemed insignificant, to him it was worth gold.

'You were a beautiful dancer.' He bent his head and cupped her face with his hands. 'But you grew up with two very sensible people who had serious, hard, demanding jobs. You *learned* to suppress your emotions, but that doesn't for a second mean they're not there. Hiding your emotions is not the same as not having them.'

CHAPTER EIGHT

ELISE KNEW IT wouldn't be showing, but on the inside she was shaking. She'd never told another person the real reason she left the Australian Ballet. Everyone had assumed it was because of her father's death, and she never bothered to correct them because it was easier than admitting such a fundamental flaw.

Now she'd blurted out the truth to Col and he wasn't running. He didn't think her vain or stupid or frivolous for the real reason. In fact, he was looking at her with such burning intensity that she wasn't sure what to do next. She had assumed the story would put him off, make him see how broken she was. But it only increased the crackling energy between them.

Suddenly her palms felt scorched against his magnificent, muscled chest. Thinking about the past had taken her mind off his physical prowess, until now. He was fair but the summer had warmed his skin to a light tan shade, dark hair dusted the tops of his forearms, the rings around his nipples and paved the way from his belly button to the well-placed knot of his towel. Her breath hitched and she withdrew her hands.

'So now you know.'

'Now I know,' he echoed. His hands dropped from

her face to the tops of her arms. It was as if he wanted to give her space but wasn't quite ready to let go yet. 'I know something real.'

She'd never felt more exposed in her whole life, including the time that her leotard strap broke in the middle of dress rehearsal *and* the time Madame Bershov gave her a public dressing-down for being late to class. She felt even more exposed than when she stood at her father's funeral and was the only person not crying.

He'd managed to get her to reveal more of herself than any other person, and he hadn't even asked for it… not directly, at least.

'You have nothing to be ashamed of, Elise. You're a wonderful person, you're caring, incredibly beautiful…'

His breath was coming heavy now, the muscles in his arms tensed. A droplet of water ran down the roped muscle of his neck and pooled at the base. Instinct took over and she leant forward, her tongue collecting the drop from his skin. He tasted fresh and clean, smelled of sandalwood soap. She pressed her lips against him, sucking on his skin before pulling back and looking up with her heart in her mouth.

'Elise.' Her name was a long, low growl on his lips.

'Shut up, Col.' She wound her hands around his neck and dragged his head down until their foreheads touched. 'I think we've talked enough.'

He pulled her to him roughly, the knot of his towel and the erection beneath digging into her belly. His mouth found hers, hot and desperate and open. His hands thrust up into her hair and he tilted her head back, kissing her as deeply as he could. The world tilted around them, the view blurring until it was a haze of golden dots on an inky piece of velvet.

'I want you, Ellie. I can't stop it.'

'Please,' she breathed. 'Don't.'

Suddenly her back was against the suite's dining table, though she'd scarcely been aware of them moving. He hoisted her up and placed her on the table, standing between her legs so the knot of his towel rubbed at her aching centre. It was at this point that she wished she'd worn a dress—her denim shorts were far too thick a barrier between them.

His mouth was at her neck, lips sucking and tongue flicking and teeth scraping. He kissed along her jaw and found her mouth again. He tasted of mint, fresh and slightly earthy. The stubble on his jaw scratched her cheek and she knew tomorrow there would be marks of him all over her.

His hand found the hem of her top and slipped underneath; she hadn't worn a bra and he palmed her so slowly she thought she might explode from impatience. Her hand found the knot of his towel and struggled to loosen it.

'Did you superglue this damn thing?' she panted, gasping as his deft fingers found her nipple.

'I'm a master towel tier.' He chuckled. 'Want a hand?'

She nodded and he stepped back, his hands dropping to the towel and slowly unravelling it. The towel dropped to the floor and all she could do was stare. He'd been amazing with the towel, but without he had a body worthy of a museum sculpture. Hard, muscular thighs extended out from narrow hips, far from the skinny boy's legs she remembered him having. His erection jutted forward, swollen and heavy-looking.

'You grew up,' she breathed, hands itching to wrap around him.

'The passage of time tends to have that effect.' His grin was sly, predatory. 'Your turn.'

She lay back against the table, her hands sliding down to find the zipper of her denim shorts. She undid them and started to slide them down her hips.

'A little help here?'

His hands tucked under the waistband and tugged; the denim slipped off and fell to the floor with a soft thud. She wriggled out of her pink and yellow cotton underwear, relishing the cool air against her burning skin.

'Touch yourself,' he demanded.

Elise bit down on her lip—she'd never masturbated in front of someone before. In fact, the only time she'd ever been able to orgasm from anything but a man's mouth had been at the hands of Col the first time around. Oral was fine—with a man's head buried between her legs they couldn't see her face, couldn't watch for the right expressions. That always made her so self-conscious.

'It's okay, Ellie. It's just me. Show me what you like.'

She'd told him why she quit ballet and he hadn't run. Maybe this wouldn't be so bad. Stalling, she ran flat palms over her smooth belly, skimming her hip bones and sweeping down the outside of her thighs. She drew a very slow line back up the inside, feeling her muscles clench as her fingertips brushed her sex. A jolt of pleasure shot through her and she gasped, her teeth clamping down on her lower lip.

'That's it.' He came closer, his clear blue eyes almost completely absorbed by the black of his pupils. 'Show me.'

She dipped her hand lower, tracing the line of her centre until she reached the tight bundle of nerves at her apex. Her back arched and a cry escaped her lips. Closing her eyes, she continued to explore herself, something she'd only ever done in the complete dark when totally alone. His lips pressed against the inside of her knee, while his hands slid under her thighs.

He kissed the line up to her, replacing her hand with his tongue. He started slowly, with maddening flicks that stoked her fire and nudged her slowly towards the edge of sanity. Her fingers tangled in his short hair and held him in place. Each movement pried her apart, the chasm within her opening until she felt as though she were about to explode.

'Please, Col. I'm so close.'

'Slowly, Ellie. I've been waiting half a decade for this,' he murmured against her, the vibrations of his voice sending ripples of pleasure through her.

She squirmed against him, the need for a too-long-absent release building steadily within her. He increased the pressure of his lips, his tongue working her perfectly. The quaking started low in her belly and flared out suddenly as she tipped over the edge, orgasm dazzling and blinding her.

She tried to sit up and look at him, but her limbs were heavy and pleasure sounds continued to emanate from the back of her throat. He stood, sliding his hands under her back and lifting her into his arms. Her hands wound around his neck and she pressed her face against his chest.

'That was…' She trailed off into a murmur.

'Amazing is the word you were looking for.'

'Cocky, aren't you?' She grinned into his chest, feeling gloriously protected and weightless.

'Hard not to be with a beautiful woman screaming your name.'

Her head snapped up. 'I didn't!'

'Yes, you did.'

The slight burning in her throat suggested he was right. She swallowed and stared wordlessly into his eyes. They were light blue, like faded denim, but ringed with a thin strip of navy. From a distance you probably wouldn't notice it, but she had these eyes permanently printed into her memory.

'You probably woke the neighbours.'

She tried to thump a fist against his chest but he dropped her onto the bed, laughing. She pulled the grey silk top she was still wearing over her head and dropped it on the floor.

'That's more like it.' He came down over her, the large expanse of his chest covering her easily.

She ran both palms up his chest, brushing his small flat nipples until she reached his shoulders. Sliding an arm under her lower back, he rolled so that she landed on top of him, straddling his hips with her thighs.

Her shoulders bunched up under her ears; she hated being on top. In fact, she was sure a previous relationship ended because she refused to be on top...or maybe it was because she insisted on having the lights off. She tried to climb down but Col's large hands held her in place.

'Where do you think you're going?'

She squirmed, wriggling her hips against his in an attempt to break free of his grip but all she did was rub herself against his erection, making him groan and press his head back against the pillow.

'I'm going to turn the light off.'

He released her and she switched off the light, frowning when she realised the glow of the city view meant real darkness would not eventuate.

'What's wrong, Ellie?'

He held a hand out and she crawled back onto the bed, snuggling against him as though it were the place she slept every night. His large arms engulfed her, and she sighed. Her heartbeat slowed to a steady rhythm.

'Are you nervous?'

'I thought we were done talking for tonight.'

He bent down and kissed her. She opened to him with terrifying ease, her tongue seeking him out instinctively.

'I need to know you're not going to go crazy in the morning.'

'Who says I'm going to make it to morning?' she teased, tracing the line of his jaw with her fingertip.

'If you think I'm letting you out of my bed before the sun comes up you've got another thing coming.' His kiss deepened, his hand finding her breasts once more.

She melted into his touch, forcing aside her insecurities and letting him play her like an instrument. He clasped his fingers around her wrist and pressed her hand to his chest.

'You can touch me, you know. I won't bite.'

'I somehow doubt that.'

She slid her hand lower, smoothing her palm along the lines of his muscles, over the bones in his hip and down to the silken strength of him. He gasped as she wrapped her hand around him, stroking the length slowly. She flicked her thumb over the tip and he growled.

His hand reached out to the side table, blindly patting around for something. His wallet. A foil packet was produced and soon he was covered and ready.

Before he had the chance to pull her on top of him, she took matters into her own hand. She tugged his arm hard and he got the hint. His thigh nudged her legs apart and he entered her in one long, careful stroke.

'Ellie.' His face burrowed into her neck, his breath hot and delicious against her skin. 'My perfect Ellie.'

Bucking her hips against him, she gave in to the haze of arousal and heard her own cries before she realised any sound had escaped her lips. A delicious and guttural sound came from the back of Col's throat as her fingernails dug into his buttocks.

He increased the tempo, his control slipping away like satin from skin. For a moment she forgot to worry about what her own face was showing, and she lost herself in the pleasure painted clearly over his. His eyes locked onto hers and his lips mouthed her name over and over.

The bubble of excitement swelled within her, ready to burst. When his lips found hers again their bodies were fused from end to end. She chased release, writhing under him as he pushed them both to ecstasy.

It wasn't until he slumped over her that she noticed the sound of her own voice ringing in her ears. She had indeed been crying out his name.

In that moment after he'd come, Col thought that the world might actually be perfect. Perhaps as a reward for all the pain he'd packed into his young life he now got to experience unadulterated happiness. Doubt niggled at him; the sensible, logical mind he'd used to dominate the technology industry told him that pure happiness was a fallacy. That life was varying in levels of imperfection, but no matter how small there was always something waiting to fail.

Elise had wriggled out from under him and was now on her side, facing the window as he spooned her. He pressed his face into her golden hair, the blinking lights from the cityscape reflecting in their golden strands. He smoothed a hand over her head, down her arm until it cupped the curve of her hip.

'I'm going to start answering the door in my towel all the time.'

She laughed, the low throaty sound making him grin in the semi-darkness. 'You might get into some interesting situations doing that. Do you get many random visitors at home?'

She rolled over to face him. In the darkness her expression was obscured by shadows and the way she ducked her head ever so slightly. Once the lights were off she was a different person. She felt more comfortable...comfortable enough to ask about his personal life at least.

'Sadly not a lot...well, not a lot who visit only to see me.'

'What do you mean?' She traced the curve of his nipple with her fingertip.

'I get a lot of up-and-coming techies wanting to pitch their latest app or game, sometimes it's a reporter wanting an interview...' He let out a sharp laugh, the humourless sound echoing in the quiet room. 'It's not often people come to visit me who aren't there because I've employed them or they were after something.'

'You always were a bit of a hermit.' She snuggled closer to him. 'Now you're a sexy hermit.'

'Is that right?' He leant down to kiss the centre of her forehead but she surprised him by tilting her face up and catching his kiss with her open mouth.

'The hermit part or the sexy part?'

'The sexy part.'

'Yes,' she purred. 'Sex on a very large stick…in my humble opinion.'

'You're not so bad yourself, Queen Bun Head.' He reached behind her and cupped her bare arse in his hands.

'I'm not really queen of the bun heads anymore.' She sighed. 'I couldn't even save my own business without help. I don't think that makes me queen of anything.'

He held his breath, waiting to see if any more words would follow. This was the most she'd ever opened up and he was reluctant to move, to breathe, to speak or to do anything else that might have her running for emotional cover.

Silence settled over them like a blanket. He waited and waited but nothing further came. 'I don't think you give yourself enough credit. You're a great role model for all those burgeoning little bun heads at the studio.'

'Hardly.'

'It's true,' he said, cupping her cheeks with his hands, forcing her face up to his. 'With all you've been through you're still fighting, still trying to get it all right.'

She screwed up her nose and tried to pull away from him, but he hooked a leg over her hip and held her close. At the sudden full-frontal body contact he felt himself stirring again and she took advantage of his arousal to distract him. Her hand slid down between them to cup his erection, and his thoughts dissolved into a groan.

'Nice try.' He ground the words out while willing

himself not to press into her palm, but her gentle strokes were doing a number on his ability to think straight. 'But that won't stop me asking questions.'

'Oh, I think it will.' She pressed her lips against the side of his jaw, her tongue flicking out to graze against his stubble. 'Eventually all your blood will head south and you'll be powerless.'

Powerless? She must be dreaming. He grabbed her shoulders and rolled them so that he was on top, pinning her hands above her head. She rolled her hips, grinding her pelvis up against his.

'I can still distract you from this angle.'

'I have no doubt you could distract me from any angle.' A surge of arousal raced through him as he looked down at the gorgeous girl beneath him. She was all pink cheeked and wide-eyed with her halo of blonde hair fanned out around her in a mess of wavy strands. 'But I want to know why you're avoiding talking to me.'

'I thought we'd got past the talking bit.' Another bump of her sex against his made his blood simmer. The girl was determined when she wanted to be.

'We're friends, Ellie. We don't ever get past the talking bit. That's kind of how it works.'

'This doesn't feel very friendly.' Her eyes gleamed, a confused mix of hope and fear rolling across her face like clouds blocking and releasing the sun. 'This feels like something else.'

She didn't know what to think. She'd come here to return his money and instead she'd confessed her sins and then taken him to bed. So much for salvaging her conscience—she was simply adding to the piles of things she'd messed up in her life.

She didn't want to have this conversation with Col; she would have been quite happy to indulge in his body until the sun came up and then never talk about it ever again. He was leaving the country at the end of the week and she had to find something else to fixate on. Having him around had proved to be a much-needed break from her usual responsibilities of the studio and taking care of her mother.

Elise bit down on her lip; she needed to check in on her mum. She made a mental note to do it as soon as she got home, and then she pushed the guilt from her mind. Didn't she deserve a little fun? She was barely twenty-seven but she was burned out. Losing herself under Col's expert touch had taken years of stress from her; now she felt young and beautiful and free.

'Talk to me, Ellie. What's going on in that pretty little head of yours?'

'I was wondering if it was greedy to try for round two.' She grinned, enjoying the way an equal smile spread over his face. His teeth gleamed in the moonlight; he'd had them fixed. Funny how she'd only just noticed that.

'And?'

'I decided I don't care if it's greedy. I want you again, Col.'

She could see he was trying to hang on, but he'd come dangerously close to getting her to open up...more than she already had. That meant she needed to get him to focus on something else, and if that focus happened to be pleasuring her then it was win-win.

'You're impossible.' He brought his mouth down to hers, hot and forceful. 'You're maddening and frustrating and...'

'And?'

'Insanely hot.'

She laughed, closing her eyes for a moment and revelling in the need that built in her. She'd forgotten how incredible sex could be. With her previous partners it had simply become another opportunity for them to see how emotionally inept she was. But with Col it was different. She felt self-conscious, sure, but there was something about his large yet gentle hands that put her at ease. He pushed her for more than she had to give, and she wished with all her heart she could give him what he needed, but even then he cared for her in a way no one else ever had.

'I like insanely hot.'

His lips came down to her neck and he kept her hands pinned above her head. He let his weight press her into the bed; trapping her, making her his prisoner. It felt primal, basal. She'd never been so close to the brink of showing who she was, of truly being herself.

She squeezed her eyes shut, as if it would create a barrier between them. But he released her hands and found her centre. Sliding his fingers into her, he brushed his thumb across her clitoris so slowly that she wanted to scream and demand more, but pleasure had rendered her helpless. All she could do was writhe and meet his slow strokes with the thrust of her hips.

He paused briefly to sheath himself with a fresh condom and before her body had time to be used to the absence of him he was back inside her. This time it was slower, deeper, and orgasm welled inside her with a force that made her shake.

As he tipped them over the edge they were barely

moving, the slow grind of his hips so languid she felt intoxicated by him.

'Come for me, Ellie.' His breath was hot against her ear. 'Don't hold back. I want to see everything you've got.'

She shook her head, but release was within her reach and she couldn't say no. Her mask slipped as the waves of orgasm built. When the full shock waves hit her she broke apart and her cry echoed high in the hotel room.

The sound of her heartbeat thumping drowned out their heavy breathing. Uneasiness settled over her. What had she done? Repeating the mistakes of her much younger, much stupider self wasn't something she'd planned on. Col would be gone at the end of the week and if for some reason he hadn't left then he most certainly would when he realised just how broken she was. An earth-shattering orgasm did not a healthy emotional relationship make.

She thought about getting up and leaving but Col's warm arms enveloped her and pulled her close against him. Her heartbeat slowed, the panicked thoughts disappeared and her mind became quiet. She relaxed into him, willing the calm to last forever.

CHAPTER NINE

A LOUD SCREECHING shocked Elise into wakefulness. Blinding sunlight streamed in through the windows, making her squint and shield her eyes with her forearm.

'What *is* that?'

'It's called an alarm.' Col's deep, husky voice sent a shiver through to the very marrow of her bones. 'A device one uses to ensure they wake up at the correct time in the morning.'

'Sounds more like a torture device if you ask me.' She pushed herself into a sitting position and rolled her shoulders. They ached with the same sense of exhausted satisfaction as the rest of her. 'Cruel and unusual torture.'

'This from the girl who used to wake up at the crack of dawn to be the first girl in the ballet studio.'

'I was young and foolish.' She pulled a mock serious face. 'I didn't appreciate a good sleep in for what it was worth.'

'I think there's a lot we didn't appreciate when we were young and foolish.' His tone was serious, the blue of his eyes piercing in the morning sun.

He'd showered and looked exactly the same as he did when he'd answered the door last night; white towel slung low on his lean hips, wet hair darkened to ebony, droplets of water scattered across his muscled shoulders. She sucked in a breath as flashing images of her nails digging into his shoulders overtook her. Liquid heat pooled low in her belly and made her limbs feel quivery. How could she possibly want him so soon after he'd satisfied her beyond her understanding of satisfaction?

'I know there are things I should have appreciated far more.'

He stalked across the room until he arrived in front of her. He dropped down to his knees and eased her back so that he could bend over her and swirl his tongue against the ridge of her hip bone. Deft fingers toyed with the edge of her underwear while his warm breath tickled her skin.

'I should have appreciated *you*, Ellie, instead of running away. I—'

'Stop it.' She planted her hands on his shoulders and pushed him back. 'Please, stop it.'

'What?'

As she sat up she was met with hurt and confusion; it was starting already. Her inability to talk about her feelings or even listen to his was forcing a wedge between them and they'd only just woken up. Her mouth felt as though it were filled with cotton balls.

'I don't want to get into this.'

'You don't want to get into this *now*?'

She wanted to swallow the rising panic that climbed dangerously high in her throat, threatening to choke her. 'I don't want to get into this full stop.'

'You're going to have to deal with it one day.' He stood up, his shadow eclipsing her.

'Says who?'

'Says the guy who's only going to be able to try for so long.' He turned and walked to the bathroom.

She wanted to shout back at him but the words stuck in her throat. He'd already left her once; he would do it again. Wasn't it better if she let him walk away now? She'd made a mistake in coming here last night but she didn't have to string it out. Like a Band-Aid, wasn't that always the advice?

'I…' Her voice faded into nothingness.

He paused at the doorway to the bathroom and turned as though he'd heard something, but when she didn't say anything he closed the door quietly behind him.

The face that stared back in the bathroom mirror was not one he'd want to inflict on anyone. Two dark brows were slashed into a downward point above his nose. His jaw was clenched and his chest rose and fell with short bursts.

He looked just like his father.

For so long Col had been able to keep his temper in check. He kept his drinking to a minimum, and avoided it altogether when he'd had a bad day. His father had always been an angry drunk and Col had done his utmost not to try his luck and see if he was the same. He'd even managed to keep his cool when a reporter had shown up at his office, questioning whether Hillam was his real last name. Obviously he hadn't buried his past far enough away; he should have chosen a name that was further from his history.

But Elise could make him feel any emotion in the book, especially the ones he didn't want to feel. Her words, the memory of her dainty hands wrapped around him and the taste of her all sent him to a place that was terrifying. She might not be able to show her own feelings, but she could conjure his as easily as if she'd hardwired straight into his brain.

He fought the urge to slam his fist against the wall. Why did he want her when she so clearly didn't want him…not beyond the physical, anyway? Was he so pathetic, so screwed up that he could only love someone who didn't love him back, who *couldn't* love him back? Was that the legacy his father had beaten into him?

He practised the breathing exercises he used whenever he felt the frustration take hold. Slow breath in, count to five, slow breath out.

'Col?'

'We need to get ready, Ellie.' He braced a hand against the door, wishing he could fling it open and sweep her up in his arms. But that wouldn't solve a damn thing.

'I'm sorry. I'm not very good at this.'

He closed his hand around the doorknob and debated whether or not to let her in.

God, if he couldn't even let her into a room, how could he possibly contemplate more?

'Don't open the door,' she said, as if reading his mind. 'Maybe I can talk a little easier if I don't have to worry about my face.'

'What are you talking about?'

'I know my face doesn't look right when I'm trying to talk about something difficult…'

'Ellie, your face is perfect.' He sighed and leant his forehead against the door. 'Your face would make a painter weep for joy.'

'Don't be sarcastic.'

'I'm not.' He really wasn't.

Elise had been the bane of her brother's existence through high school. Every guy wanted to date her and Rich had shooed them all away with a threat…even him. At times he'd felt sorry for Rich. Elise had been the better student, the more popular sibling, she'd been a ballet star and was gorgeous to boot. She seemed to win out on every single facet of life.

'What I mean is that I don't show emotions properly on my face.'

Col felt awareness run through him, as if a piece of the puzzle had finally clicked into place. 'Who on earth told you that?'

'Well, they always said it at ballet.' She paused. 'But I was dating this guy, and he said my face was like a brick wall.'

Silence. Col swallowed down anger that flared like the lighting of a match within him. Getting angry would not help Elise.

'Well, that guy was clearly doing something wrong then, because I saw every little bit of feeling on your face last night.'

'He's right. I don't do the emotional stuff very well.'

'I'm opening this door.' He grabbed the handle and let himself out of the bathroom.

Shock flickered across her face for a split second, but then her eyes hardened and her mouth pushed into a flat line. He knew that face—it was her game face. The one she used when she felt threatened or unsure or vulnerable. And he knew she would be feeling all three of those things right now.

'The guy that said that to you had no idea what he was talking about.' He cupped her face between his hands and held her steady when she tried to twist away.

'I see you, Ellie. I see what's going on in your head…
There's *nothing* wrong with you.'

She bit down on her lip and looked at him, the mask
firmly in place. He'd lost her as soon as he'd opened
that door when she'd asked him not to.

'Well, anyway,' she said, her voice perky and a smile
firmly painted on. 'It's your day to today. As you said,
it's time to get ready.'

'And what exactly are you going to wear?' He looked
at the T-shirt she'd plucked from his luggage, his eyes
lingering on where the soft grey fabric skimmed the
tops of her toned thighs.

Her underwear was hanging from the armchair in the
corner of the room and her silky top was in a rumpled
heap on the floor. There was no way she'd have time
to go home and get changed; they had to improvise.

'This?' She looked down at the T-shirt and back up
at him. 'Or not?'

'Don't think I've forgotten about our conversation.'
He leant down and pressed his forehead to hers, hurt
searing the inside of his chest when a flicker of fear
passed over her eyes. 'We're going to continue it tonight.'

'Says who?' She crossed her arms across her chest,
causing the T-shirt to rise and almost expose the place
he'd explored so intimately last night.

He swallowed and pushed aside the hot, achy feeling that was causing him to swell. He had neither the
time nor the headspace to deal with his inconvenient
feelings towards Elise Johnson.

'Says me.' He strode to the cupboard and pulled out
his clothes, throwing them on before tossing Elise a
white cotton shirt. 'If you roll the sleeves up this might

be okay. As for your underwear, I can't help you with that. You'll have to go commando.'

She picked up her denim shorts and slipped them on, looking up at him as she did so. Was someone up there trying to punish him? How on earth would he be able to concentrate all day knowing Elise was wearing his shirt and *not* wearing anything beneath those tiny shorts? Cruel it was, just cruel.

She slipped the T-shirt off over her head and he caught a glimpse of bare breast before she wriggled into the shirt, tied it at the waist and rolled the sleeves up. The white cotton against faded denim made her skin glow, and with her blonde hair all messed up she looked nothing short of a fantasy.

'Ready?' She grabbed her bag and started out towards the main room.

'I don't think I'll ever be ready,' he muttered under his breath.

By the time they made it to the convention centre, which was conveniently placed across the road, the lines were already circling the venue and the noise was rising. This particular conference wasn't quite as crazy as some of the ones he'd attended in the US earlier in his career. There weren't as many people in costume and the crowds were smaller. But the buzz filled the air with a palpable excitement and Col's stomach flipped when he realised how big that auditorium would feel when it was full.

Perspiration beaded at his brow and suddenly Col's mouth was drier than a drought-ravaged field. His heart rate climbed and each breath felt harder and more forced. He was about to distract himself with inane con-

versation when Elise took his hand and squeezed. She
didn't turn to look at him; she didn't say a word. She
simply held his hand and the simplicity of her action
said more than any words or look could have.

They slipped through the VIP entrance to the conference, and the main hall was abuzz with the stall holders
preparing for opening time. They had ten minutes to go
and there was plenty of last-minute scrambling to make
sure that everything was perfect. The Hillam Technologies stall was in the far corner, gleaming displays of
their latest apps and software programs—mainly personal fitness and health apps with gamification ele-
ments—set up and ready to go.

'Did you make all of these?' Elise peered at the dis-
play devices, swiping and tapping at the apps to test
them out. '*Run for your life*, what's that about?'

'Ah, but only the most fun and creative running app
around.' Col swiped at the iPad and took the app back
to its home screen. 'It's a running app with different
survival themes. There's a zombie apocalypse, bear attack, escape from the jungle—'

'Why on earth would anyone want to pretend they
were being chased by a bear?'

'If it motivates people to run faster, harder, longer...'
he paused, enjoying the tint of colour spreading across
Elise's cheeks '...then it's good for fitness. That's one
of our philosophies: we create apps to take the boring
out of everyday activities.'

'Mr Hillam?' One of the young guys behind the stand
approached them, hand outstretched. 'I'm Brody. So
nice to meet you in person finally.'

Col took in the spiked black hair and colourful sleeve
tattoos on both arms. The boy might have looked as

though he'd fit right in with a rock-band road crew, but he was one of the most gifted app designers Col had ever worked with. To date they'd only ever conversed via various forms of technology since Brody was based in New Zealand.

'Yes.' Col grabbed his hand and shook it heartily. 'Much better than our usual Skype meetings. I'm glad you were able to fly out.'

'It's just a hop over the water.' He smiled.

'This is Elise Johnson.' He tried to think quick—how would one categorise their relationship? 'She's a very old and dear friend.'

'And of course by old, he means we've been friends a long time.' Elise shook Brody's hand and rolled her eyes at Col. 'You've got a way with words, Col.'

'What?' He shrugged. 'You don't look a day over sixteen.'

Elise shook her head. 'Creepy.'

'Nineteen?'

She grimaced and pointed her index finger in the air. 'Twenty-one.'

'Perfect.' A pleased smile spread across her lips and she turned back to Brody. 'How did you come to work for Col if you're based in New Zealand?'

'I applied to the Hillam Technologies' Bright Things programme last year. Every year they run a competition and the person with the best app gets an opportunity to pitch it for sale and sometimes there's even a job offer at the end. I was one of the lucky ones.' Brody grinned. 'We don't have many large technology companies in New Zealand, so this was a dream come true.'

Warmth spread through Col's chest. He'd promised himself many times over the years—when the Johnsons had taken him in, when his bank manager had given him a chance with a small business loan—that one day he would pay it forward. The Bright Things programme offered smart kids the opportunity to kickstart their career in technology. Winners were assigned a mentor and often the company bought the app the student had pitched. In fact, some of their top-selling apps had come from this programme.

The winner of the first year had already left Hillam Technologies to start his own venture, and Col couldn't have been happier for him. Each time he helped one of these kids he felt as if he was taking another step away from his past, continually proving to himself that he was nothing like his father.

'Wow.' Elise grinned and looked up at Col, genuine pride shining from her grey eyes. 'That's so wonderful.'

She reached down and squeezed his hand and Col had to force himself not to think about how naked she was under his shirt and her tattered denim shorts. No bra, no underwear. Luckily his shirt was a heavy weave, meant for the frosty air conditioning of an office, and so none of her small, golden breasts showed through. But he knew and that was enough.

Col suddenly felt hot and bothered; he slipped off his linen blazer and slung it over one arm. 'We should probably get over to the auditorium. I'm the first speaker of the day, so I want to get out of here before the crowds arrive.'

As he took Elise's hand again, they heard the rush of the crowd; the event was open. Bidding Brody and the others on the Hillam Technologies stand good luck, they exited back through the VIP area and found themselves in the entrance of the convention building.

The crowds were bigger now, the noise louder. Even the reassuring sensation of Elise's palm on his wasn't enough to quell the nausea that overtook him with force. He had only half an hour to get to the presenters' lounge and that meant it was only an hour before he'd be on stage. The very thought of it made the bile rise up in his throat, and he swallowed it back by breathing long and slow.

'So I'm an old and dear friend, am I?'

Col rolled his eyes. 'You know I didn't mean physically old. You women are so sensitive.'

'Do you do what we did last night with all your *old, dear* friends?'

It was easy to sink back into the memory, images flickering like a reel of photographs before him. Hands, lips, tongues, curves. They were all there, now permanently etched into his memory...which was a good thing considering how their morning had gone back at the hotel room. He'd lose her soon, and memories would be all he'd have.

'Considering my only other dear, old friends are your brother and my head of PR, the answer to that question would be no.'

'There's only three of us?' She looked up at him, fair brows knitted above two saucer-like grey eyes. Were her eyes bigger today or was it just that he'd seen beneath the surface last night?

'That's it, I'm afraid. Quality over quantity.'

She nodded, satisfied. 'Well, I'm glad to be your dear old friend who sometimes has sex with you.'

'Sometimes?'

'Twice,' she corrected.

'Exactly. It needs to be more than twice to qualify

for "sometimes".' Col stopped short of the presenters' lounge and opened the door for her. 'Sometimes is at least seven.'

'Seven?' She laughed, shaking her head and brushing past him.

'It could even be as high as ten…or thirteen.'

'Don't push your luck.'

The presenters' lounge was small, more of a holding area than a room. The walls were cream, two couches the colour of milky coffee faced one another and there was a vase of fresh flowers on a glass coffee table. It looked calm, perfectly lacking in personality.

Col pushed his sweat-slicked palms down the front of his jeans. He pulled the note cards from the pocket on the inside of his jacket, which was creased from being folded over one arm.

'Leave it with me.' Elise extended her hand and took the jacket from him. 'It'll be hot on stage with all those lights—you won't need a jacket.'

He tapped a maddening beat with one sneaker-clad foot and undid the top button of his shirt. Why had he agreed to do this? Nervous energy raced through him. He should have brought a stress ball, a Rubik's Cube… anything. He needed to keep his hands busy.

Tap, tap, tap. What if he got out there and no one had turned up for his talk? Worse, what if everyone had? What if he tripped while he was walking onto the stage? What if—?

'Cut it out.' Elise's voice rang sharp and loud in the quiet room.

Col's head snapped up. She was perched on the arm of the couch in front of him, long legs crossed at the ankles.

'I can hear your brain from here. Getting wound up is not going to help you.'

'I don't know what else to do,' he snapped. The fear was making him edgy, cranky.

'Just breathe.' She stood up and walked over to him, placing a hand on each of his wrists and pulling him down so that they were seated next to one another. 'Breathe in, one, two, three. Out, one, two, three.'

He followed her, sucking a bigger lungful of air each time until his heartbeat slowed. He felt like a fool, being so worked up over such a small thing. Over something that no one else seemed to take issue with. He'd done so much with his life. He'd travelled the world and made a very successful company. He'd escaped a tyrant of a father and created a life for himself. But he couldn't even *think* about getting up on stage without having a meltdown. It was stupid, pathetic—

'I said *stop it*.' Her hands came up to his face and held him so that he could look nowhere else but her. 'You know what you're doing—you have this, Col. Everything will go fine, I promise.'

He didn't say anything. He had the urge to push her away, to tell her to leave and to lock himself away in the presenters' room until it was too late for him to go out on stage. But being a coward was not an option, not when he'd promised himself that he would never be a failure like dear, old Dad. No, he had to do this... even if it did feel as if the world were about to swallow him whole.

'And you know what else?' she said. 'I will be there in the front row. So you can look at me and pretend there's no one else in the room.'

That would be easy enough to do—whenever she

was near it felt as if reality itself slipped out of his grasp. She was here for him. He tried to ignore the tiny flare of hope in his chest at the way she looked at him, so open, so encouraging. He knew it couldn't last; as soon as things got tough she would shut down... She always did.

He sighed, pushing himself up from the couch. The event coordinator had come into the room and was calling him to come through to the auditorium.

Elise leaned in and gave him a kiss, her lips pressed firmly against his. Taken aback, Col watched mutely as she darted out of the room to find her place in the auditorium ahead of his arrival. Col stepped through the door after her, walking slowly, gathering himself.

The conference organiser's voice boomed through the auditorium speakers. 'He's one of the most successful men in technology under thirty. He sold his first computer application design at the age of twenty-two and had made his first billion by twenty-eight. Little is known about him since, like most technologists, he prefers to tinker with his toys instead of talking about himself. But he's here today in a rare public appearance. Ladies and gentlemen, I present to you CEO of Hillam Technologies, Col Hillam.'

As he walked up the steps to the stage area, the lights dazzled him, stealing his focus momentarily. The auditorium was not just full, it was *heaving*. People were standing at the back where there were no seats, and they were still trickling in.

For a moment he was worried the world would go black. The floor seemed to tilt under him as the man who'd introduced him shook his hand. But he saw her, sitting in the front row. She leant forward so that her forearms rested on her knees, her head nodding at him. *You can do it.*

CHAPTER TEN

WATCHING COL UP on stage was surreal, especially knowing how he really felt about being in the spotlight. Despite his fear, he owned the stage as Elise knew he would. He looked like a force to be reckoned with, his deep voice filling the room, commanding attention.

Once he got into his talk his face became animated, his eyes lit up and he talked with all the passion she knew to be in him. He got the crowd to laugh, got them to nod their heads and had them—especially the women—eating out of the palm of his hand.

Pride surged through her as she watched him draw his speech to a close. He stood in the centre of the stage, long legs encased in dark denim, his black shirt showcasing a broad chest and shoulders. His silver ID bracelet glinted as it caught the light. Elise swallowed, her mouth dry.

As he closed off his talk the crowd roared their approval, the applause deafening her. He unclipped the microphone from his shirt collar and shook the hand of the man who'd introduced him earlier. As he started to descend the steps of the stage, a small crowd of people gathered around him. Elise hung back, unsure whether to break through and claim her space next to him. She didn't really deserve that spot, not after the way she'd treated him this morning.

His eyes flickered to hers and he motioned her over. Relieved not to have to make the decision herself, she went to him.

'You'll have to excuse me, folks,' he said, grabbing her hand as she broke through the crowd, 'but I'm due on the Hillam Technologies booth now. Thanks for coming to see me.'

'Just one more question, Mr Hillam.' A woman with a hard-edged voice thrust a recorder in his direction. 'Is it true that Hillam is not your real name?'

Elise sucked in a breath. Col paled for a brief moment, the torment he normally kept hidden flashed across his face. But then the mask was on, the charming, gleaming-toothed smile firmly in place and his voice was smooth as honey.

'Can't a man have a little mystery about himself?' He shrugged and gave a little laugh. 'Truth is I thought it sounded better than my family name. It's nothing more sinister than a little marketing.'

The reporter didn't look satisfied with his answer but Col nodded and moved away from the crowd, his hand holding hers in a vice-like grip. Elise could feel the tremor in his arm, the twitching muscles that told her he was doing his best to hold the anger and fear in. She knew better than to believe the face he presented to the world; she knew him…more than anyone.

'Have they cottoned on?' she asked as they slipped out of the auditorium and through one of the side entrances.

Outside, sunshine was pouring down. A gentle breeze shook the trees and threw dappled light across the small patch of garden that sat between them and South Wharf boardwalk. People milled about, music wafted over from an open-air bar on the river's edge, and the *Polly Woodside* sat regally in its permanent home.

'Ever since I arrived my assistant has been fielding questions from Australian journalists about my origins.' He sighed, toying with his bracelet. They dropped down onto a wooden bench, and Col raked a hand through his hair. 'There was only the odd question about life in Australia when I was in the States, but ever since I came home...'

'You did the right thing by coming home.'

He nodded. 'I know.'

'You were amazing out there on that stage.' She touched a hand to his knee. 'I'm really proud of you.'

He looked at her, unmoving. He was wound up, shoulders tensed and the muscles in his neck seemed stiff. She could see nothing in his eyes, no flicker of emotion, no truth. Her stomach churned; she'd seen his mask many times over the years but it was never before directed at her. He was always open with her, always.

This is what it must feel like for anyone who tries to care about you.

'What's wrong, Col?'

'I'm fine.' He shifted so that she had to withdraw her hand. 'But it's been a very long week.'

'Are you looking forward to going home?'

She wasn't sure she wanted to know the answer to this. Wouldn't it be easier if he left? She could get on with her life, get on with making sure her studio was on track. That was all she wanted...wasn't it?

'Yeah, I've got so much work on. It'll be good to

go home and get a bit of distance from all this. Hopefully the journos won't bother me once I'm out of the country again.'

She wanted to ask if he'd miss her when he left, if he missed her last time he left. But the words wouldn't come; they lodged in her throat and made it hard to breathe. She frowned and watched a boy skateboard past with his dog running next to him. They looked so happy and free.

'We should probably get inside.' Col stood. 'Although you're relieved of your duties if you want to go home.'

She blinked at him. 'Relieved of my duties?'

'Yeah. The speech is done and dusted—that's what I paid you for.' He looked past her as he spoke, his words forcing a gulf between them. 'That's what I needed.'

Her initial reaction would have been to let him shut her out—after all, it saved her from doing it to him later on. But something deep inside her made her hold her ground. Like a magnetic force it kept her next to him.

'I'd like to stay,' she said, not missing his curious glance and almost imperceptible lift of his lips. 'Missy has taken over all of my classes for the day, so I can help out with your stand if you like?'

'I'll give you a crash course in technology.' He motioned for her to go through the door before him, his hand finding the small of her back as they walked through to the conference's VIP entrance.

'Start with a low base,' she said.

'There's this thing called the internet—'

She whacked his arm with the back of her hand and he laughed. The booming sound filled her chest, warmed her cheeks and made her blood pump faster.

'Not *that* low.'

By the time the conference drew to a close Elise's feet were throbbing, her face ached from hours of smiling and she felt more gloriously happy and satisfied than she had felt in a long time. Watching Col at work was a magical thing. Talking to the young developers who were interested in his product and his company, he was truly alive. He'd even handed out his business card to a few of the stand-out young techies and told them to call him when they were out of university and looking for work.

Col's head of PR, Pete, was finishing up at the stand, talking to a few technology bloggers about Hillam Technologies' up-and-coming products. But as far as the conference was concerned, it was done and dusted.

'How does it feel to be king of the technology castle?' She leant back against a wall in the corridor where she and Col had snuck off to for a little privacy.

'Since the day I moved in with your family I knew I would make it here,' he said, taking her hand and pulling her to him.

'Why is that?'

'Because I was finally surrounded by people who thought I was more than a punching bag.'

Elise bit down on her lip, trying to shield herself from the painful memories. Even all these years later she remembered him, battered and bruised. The boy who wore his armour everywhere…everywhere except when he was with her.

'Your family saved me, Ellie. I'm king of the castle because of *you*.'

She didn't know what to say, so instead she threw her arms around his neck and dragged his head down to herself for a deep, searching kiss. Blood rushed in her ears, goosebumps rippled across her body as he drew her closer. Crushing her body to his.

They only broke apart when the sound of cameras clicking pulled their attention away from the kiss. A few kids wearing media passes had their cameras and smartphones aimed at Col and Elise.

'Come on,' he growled in her ear. 'I think it's time for us to take this somewhere else.'

Half an hour later they were seated in the hotel bar, drinks in front of them. Col's head was spinning, and it wasn't leftovers from confronting his biggest fear. He'd been ready to cut ties with Elise when they were outside the convention centre. After the reporter had asked him about his past he'd wanted to run.

If he was linked to his father's financial crimes then his company could take a hit. Arthur Hill had been into many illegal things, but fraud was what he was most known for. With social media having the ability to spread news like wildfire, the revelation of his family secrets *and* the lies he'd told in changing his name could mean a massive loss of support for his company. He'd be stressed, working hours on end to save his company from the wasteland of his past. Would Elise stick by him through all that?

To his surprise she'd stayed on through the day of her own accord, even after he'd given her an out. Now he was conflicted—he wanted her with a force that surpassed anything he'd ever felt before. It even surpassed what he'd felt for Elise herself in the past.

However, even if nothing came of the reporter's question he'd still have to leave in a few days. His father's funeral was tomorrow and he couldn't stay longer. And *she* couldn't leave her mother…even if she did have feelings strong enough to make her so inclined. But that was the problem: he still didn't know how she felt. Every time he asked she clammed up.

It was hopeless. He should have walked away today; he should have cut the cord when he had the chance… It would have been easier for them both.

'Don't look so serious,' she said. 'The world isn't about to end, you know.'

She still wore his shirt, and as she leaned towards him he got a flash of light gold skin. Memory struck him and his eyes dropped to her shorts. He thought about how easy it would be to tuck a finger under the hem of one leg and touch her. *You're not helping yourself.*

'Hmm, that was a stark change of thought if I ever saw one.' She laughed. 'Your face just went from super serious to super turned on.'

'How can you tell?' He dragged his eyes away from her legs and up to her sparkling grey eyes.

'Your eyes get all wide when you're turned on.' She grinned slyly. 'Plus there's always one sure-fire way to tell.'

Her hand dropped into his lap and gently traced the outline of his burgeoning erection. He stiffened under her touch and had to bite back a groan.

'Yes, well…' He sighed as she squeezed him. 'That is a dead giveaway.'

'I shouldn't sleep with you again.' She raked her eyes up and lingered on the open collar of his shirt for a second.

'It certainly looks as though you feel that way,' he

said, sarcasm colouring his tone as he looked down at her hand, still in his lap.

She snatched it back, cheeks flushed. 'I should have learnt my lesson the first time.'

'And what lesson was that?' He sipped his drink.

She ran her fingers up and down the stem of her martini glass. 'That multiple orgasms tend to cloud my judgement.'

Col swallowed. 'Multiple orgasms are *never* a bad thing.'

'No, but they do have a way of obscuring the facts.'

'The facts?'

'That you and I shouldn't have got together.' She licked her lips, that pink tongue once again darting out to betray her.

'Your lips are saying one thing but I know your tells, Ellie.'

'You know far less than you think you do.' She leant forward, her hand at the collar of his shirt. 'But I know when to call your bluff.'

He breathed in the honeyed scent of her; it was complex and intoxicating. 'You certainly grew up.'

She threw her head back and laughed, the tinkling sound making his blood fizz. 'That tends to happen with the passage of time, Col.'

He smiled upon hearing his words on her lips. Col could have any woman he wanted, especially in the States where women were able to smell his wealth a mile off. Initially, he'd indulged himself with a few of the wannabe Silicon Valley wives, but he was now tired of people who were only interested in his money. Over the last twelve months he'd turned in on himself, focusing on work and pulling away from the social scene he'd grown to hate. The incident with Tessa Bates had only exacerbated his need for privacy. There was no way he'd put himself in the firing line of the paparazzi ever again.

Being here reminded him of exactly why he'd shied away from relationships. They were messy and confusing, but the thought of ever sleeping with another woman made him recoil on the inside. Elise Johnson had been his first love and he was quite certain she'd be his last.

If only he could convince her to open up. He had to know how she felt; he couldn't put himself on the line otherwise.

'Get that look off your face.' She smirked, one hand toying with a strand of hair that had come loose.

'What look?'

'The look that says you're plotting something,' she replied with a knowing smile. 'Plot on your own time.'

He finished off the last of his Scotch and waved away the bartender who'd offered him a refill. Rolling up the sleeves on his lightweight cotton shirt, he felt as if his skin were burning from the inside out.

'Still the bossy boots, that's what I like about you.' He leant forward and ran his fingertip up the length of her arm, smiling as her skin rippled with goosebumps. Good to see he had the same effect on her as she had on him. 'You're not into me for my money.'

She smiled. 'I'm not into you at all.'

'What was last night all about, then?'

'Basic human need,' she replied, but her voice was high pitched. 'Nothing more. We're friends.'

'Friends who—'

'Yes.' She cut him off, squirming in her seat. 'Not all women want love and marriage and babies, Col.'

'No, not all women do.' He watched her closely, watched for the tiny signs he was breaking through to her. 'But you do.'

'No, I don't.'

'Okay, so come up to my suite and we'll order dinner and have sex and you can go on pretending there's nothing here.' He would bide his time, then he'd ask her again and if she couldn't open up then he would call it quits. For good. 'I don't know about you but I'm starving and room service does a good steak.'

She sucked on her lower lip, her eyes narrowed at him. If she didn't agree then Col would claim victory on catching her out, if she did accept...well, then she'd be walking straight into the lion's den.

Win, win.

'Sure.' She pierced him with her sparkling grey eyes and a defiant tilt of her chin. 'I love steak.'

What in the world was she thinking?

As she walked beside Col along the opulent hallway that led to his hotel room her stomach clenched. She'd tried to play it cool and now he'd called her bluff. She'd tried to tell him she didn't want the happy Hollywood ending, that she was satisfied with sex and sex only. But nothing could be farther from the truth...she wanted it all.

Dammit.

Playing games with Col Hillam was not something she should be doing, yet the back and forth was like a drug. One she should stay the hell away from.

'I can hear the cogs in your brain turning from here.'
His deep baritone jolted her to the present.

The hallway was silent, making all the more obvious
her forced, even breathing. She hoped that the thunder-
ing of her heart couldn't be heard, nor the rushing of
her blood as she maintained a respectable distance from
Col while they walked. If she reached out and touched
him she'd surely be zapped.

He swiped the card against the panel on the door and
pushed it open, motioning with his other hand for her to
go ahead. She could feel his eyes on her as she entered
in front of him, her skin burning where the cotton of
his shirt brushed seductively against her.

Though she'd already seen it the view still struck
her with full force. The glittering lights of Melbourne
swept along the room's length in a dizzying spectacle
of colour.

Col came up close behind Elise, his presence making her bare skin under his shirt tingle with awareness.
Her nipples beaded, pushing against the soft cotton. His
breath came in hot bursts against the back of her neck,
making her body throb with need.

'It's just sex,' she warned him.

'Right.' It came out as a growl, the sound and emotion reverberating against her neck as his lips hovered
close without touching.

His hands skimmed her hips, sliding over her curves
as though he were born purely to touch her. Without
thinking, without deciding, without rationalising she
arched. Her bottom came into contact with him and if
there'd been any doubt of his feelings towards her, they
were clarified with the hard press of his arousal.

'Elise.' The 's' came out as a hiss of appreciation

and his fingers splayed against her hip bones, pulling her hard against him.

Heat gathered between her thighs, a desperate ache settling there. She longed to grab his hands and put them where she needed release, make him feel how much she'd missed him in only one day since they were last in his bed. She bit down on her lip; her head lolled to the side and rested against the hard wall of his chest.

What had happened last time she decided to see if Col's flame was as hot as it looked? She'd got burned, scarred and permanently disfigured on the inside. She couldn't go back there...again.

Yet his hands on her brought all the memories from last night flooding back. The image of him above her, his blue eyes engulfed in mirrored ecstasy, would haunt her forever.

A knock on the door caused Elise to jump, stumbling forward as Col left her and stalked to the door. A room-service cart appeared with two silver serving trays and a bottle of red wine. Col tipped the waiter and wheeled the cart towards her.

'When did you order this?' Elise planted her hands on her hips.

'About four o'clock this afternoon.' He grinned, shoving a hand through his short dark hair. 'I got a Red Hill Pinot Noir. You love a Peninsula red if memory serves me correctly.'

Elise wasn't sure whether to be furious at Col for being so presumptuous, or furious at herself for being so damn predictable. He knew she wouldn't back down from a challenge and she'd eaten right out of his hand.

She opened her mouth to snap at him when he lifted

the silver lids and a stream of delicious steak scents wafted out. 'Oh, God, I am *so* hungry.'

'Fighting or medium-rare steak…what'll it be?'

She sighed. 'Steak.'

'Excellent choice.' He held out a plate containing a very delectable-looking steak and a pile of greens.

'You're a real piece of work, you know.'

'No need to get angry.' He followed her to the coffee table and brought the wine with two glasses. He poured the glowing red liquid without spilling a drop. 'It's not my fault you can't stay away. That feels like more than sex to me.'

'I have needs.' She sliced off a piece of steak and speared it with her fork. 'You're…good.'

Real articulate there, Johnson.

'Good?' he asked, his brow raised. 'Samaritans are good. What we did last night was not…good.'

He said the word as though it left a bad taste in his mouth.

'Fulfilling.'

'Try again.' Col sliced into the tender meat, cutting off a bite-sized piece and lifting it to his mouth.

'Do you really want to talk about it?'

'Yes.'

'It was…' She trailed off. 'Spectacular.'

'Now you're getting warmer.'

He took a hearty gulp of his wine and she had to stifle the urge to kiss the flavour from his mouth. He'd undone another button on his shirt and his skin gleamed with summer heat. In the muted lighting of the hotel room he looked gorgeous, but with the restless beauty of a caged exotic animal. The fancy hotels weren't him, she knew that. He was stifled by his lifestyle, but so determined to make something of himself that he put up with it.

'Col…' She wanted to open up; there was so much to tell him.

She was cut short by the buzzing of his phone. To her surprise her brother's face flashed up onto the screen. Had they kept in touch the whole five years after he moved to the States? Had they talked and confided in one another while she'd heard not a word from him the whole time?

Col hesitated. He looked at her and she pressed her lips together, holding the words in. Grabbing the phone from the table, he tapped at the screen to answer it. Before a word had even come out of his mouth, Elise could hear the lecture from the other end of the line.

'What are you talking about?' he asked, rolling his eyes and shaking his head as her brother continued his tirade.

Col said nothing while he crossed the room and opened his laptop. Soon a search page of images filled the screen and Elise wandered over to see what the fuss was about. There were pictures of them kissing in the hallway at the conference, already uploaded for the world to see. Some were blurred iPhone snaps but others were sharp and clear. His hand was tangled in her hair and their bodies fused together.

'I know what you told me, Rich,' Col snapped. 'But she's an adult and so am I.'

More yelling on the other end. Confused, Elise turned to Col and stuck her hand out, demanding the phone. He brushed her away and turned to the wall, the phone still at his ear.

'This is ridiculous. You need to calm down. I'm not taking any of this crap from you anymore.'

When he turned Elise grabbed the phone from his hands. 'Rich, what the hell is going on?'

'Where are you?' The voice of her older brother came down the line, tinged with a hint of the English accent he'd picked up from living over there for the last few years.

'I'm with Col.'

'Where?'

She could practically see his face. He would be red-cheeked and his pale eyes would be alight but his voice was sharp and ice-like. Each word was spoken with frosty precision; he had a kind of chilling detachment when he was angry.

'In his hotel room.' She shook her head. 'I don't understand—what's the matter?'

'The matter *is*, little sister, that I told our dear friend Col to stay the hell away from you. I warned him when we were young, I warned him again after he broke the rules and now I'm doing it for the third time.'

'You told him to stay away from me.' Understanding spread through her like poison, deadening her limbs and making her head heavy. She shouldn't have been surprised; it was just like Rich. After all, he'd told her not to kiss Col. It shouldn't come as a shock that he'd had the same conversation from the other angle.

The night before Col left he'd come to her, wanting to know how she felt, needing something from her that she wasn't able to give. He'd wanted her to open up, to be vulnerable to him... He'd wanted to know if she was worth fighting for.

'Yes, I was trying to protect you. It's what a big brother should do. It's what *he* should have done.'

'He's not my brother, you are.'

Rich let out an angry huff on the other end of the line. 'That's exactly why I told him to stay away.'

'I can speak for myself. I don't need you looking after me. I've done all right ever since you bailed on Mum and I.'

'That's not fair, Ellie.' The strain in his voice came through loud and clear; she'd got him there. 'His family is no good. You deserve so much better.'

'You're right, Rich. I *do* deserve better. I deserve to have a brother who would stick by me, who would be happy for me to end up with someone as amazing as Col.'

In the silence her brother's anger simmered. Her eyes flickered to Col. He stood at the window with his back to her, hands clasped behind him.

'I didn't want you to get hurt, Ellie.' There was a long sigh on the other end of the line.

'He was your best friend, Rich. You should have been happy for us.' Now that the shock had worn off Elise's blood boiled. Her brother had been controlling, even when they were kids, but this was ridiculous.

'Happy for you to end up with him? He was *my* friend, Elise. Mine!'

Her chest constricted. Sibling rivalry had been a bit of an issue in their house growing up. Her brother had a competitive streak that could rival that of an Olympic athlete.

'You never did want to share your toys, did you?' She rolled her eyes. 'I should have guessed.'

'I always had to play second fiddle to you,' he

sneered. 'You were always practising your ballet in the lounge room, wanting everyone's attention. You were always the good little girl, Daddy's angel.'

Her stomach twisted. It seemed that Rich thought she'd taken more than her share of their parents' very limited attention growing up, and then she'd taken his best friend as well.

'But that wasn't enough, was it? Oh, no, you couldn't just be the star at home but you had to go after Col too.'

'Well, it looks like the truth has come out. This was never about whether you believed Col was good enough for me, was it? You would rather lose him altogether than share him with me.'

There was silence on the other end of the line and Elise knew she'd finally found the true motivation for her brother's actions.

'You lost the right to pass judgement when you left me here to deal with Mum all on my own,' she continued. 'Frankly, there's no place I'd rather be than with Col right now. So I'm afraid you're going to have to get over your issues with it.'

She hung up the phone. Rich, like her, wasn't very good at expressing his feelings but that didn't give him the right to interfere with her life. She could see now, with a few more years of maturity and this recent revelation on her side, that Col had wanted her permission to stay all those years ago. Only he hadn't known how to ask the question and she sure as hell hadn't been equipped to answer it.

'What did he say to you?' she asked.

'You heard him.' Col spat the words out without turning around. 'He thinks I'm trouble, no good…certainly not good enough for you.'

'I meant after we slept together…the first time.' Her tongue was heavy in her mouth, nerves on high alert. But she had to know why he left, the real reason.

'He said if I ever touched you again he'd make me pay for it. He'd tell your dad how I violated everything they'd given me, every ounce of support and care. He said they'd never want to have anything to do with me if they knew.'

She swallowed. 'But you left it all behind anyway.'

'I couldn't be in the same house with you and not feel the way I did.' He turned to her, dark brows crinkled. He rubbed a hand along his jaw. 'It was easier to put myself out of temptation's way than stay and fight it. Better to let your parents think I was off following my dreams than know that I'd screwed their daughter.'

He said it with such a harsh edge that Elise winced.

'We never *screwed*, Col.'

'Are you trying to tell me it was something more? You've spent the whole evening telling me how this is only about the sex. If that's not screwing I don't know what is.'

'Don't take this out on me, Colby Hill.'

'Hillam,' he corrected. 'The Hill name is officially dead. And you're right, it's not your fault, it's mine. I should never have come to you for help.'

'Then why did you?'

'Because I haven't been able to stop thinking about you.' He was almost shouting, his eyes flashing. 'Because I put a whole ocean between us and it wasn't enough.'

Her heart wanted to crack, it wanted to fracture straight down the middle for the anguish in his voice… the anguish she could never match on the outside. But she felt it deep down in her bones. She felt it the way she'd never felt anything else, not even when her father died, not even when she collected her mother from hospital after a bookie broke her arm. She'd shoved it all down until the hurt, the fear, the pain were as dense as concrete within her.

But the time she'd spent with Col had driven a stake into the past, causing bits of it to break off and float freely within her. She'd started to feel again.

She threw herself at him, arms and legs wrapping around him, mouth on his. She wanted to consume him, to draw in his passion and love and make it her own. She might not be able to say what was going on in her head, but she could show him with her body.

'You can't keep kissing with me to avoid talking to me.' Col drew his lips away from hers but his hands didn't let go of her.

'You want me to stop?'

'I want you to do both, Ellie.' He backed her up until her arse pressed against the cool glass of the hotel window. 'Talking *and* kissing.'

'But I'm so much better at kissing.' She demonstrated by working her way back to his mouth, tugging on his lower lip with her teeth and grinding against him.

'I need more than kissing.'

His lips came down to the crook of her neck, sucking at the delicate hollow. Her skin burned as though she were about to go up in flames. He tore at the shirt, not even bothering to undo the buttons, instead ripping it open with passionate force. His hands found her breasts and she let her head loll back against the window. His lips took one of her nipples, the pressure sending heat spiralling down to her centre.

'I can't give you both, Col.' Her breathing came fast and heavy as his hands dipped to her shorts. 'That's not how I am.'

CHAPTER ELEVEN

AFTER ANOTHER NIGHT with Elise Johnson in his bed, Col was no closer to breaking through to her. Rather than do the right thing, he'd allowed himself to give in to the insatiable desire that took hold whenever she was near. He was cheating her and he was cheating himself.

He tilted his head to the side and his neck muscles protested. He'd slept at a funny angle, not wanting to move or disturb Elise as she'd clung to him in the middle of the night. He didn't want to risk her shifting away from him when this was likely the last time he'd ever hold her in his arms.

Dammit. Thumping a fist down on the couch, he gritted his teeth. He would have to move on. He would have to go home, throw himself back into his work and give up on the fantasy that he could have it all. He couldn't have Elise, and without her there was no point trying to be with anyone else—at least not in any permanent sense.

There were plenty of men who chose the bachelor lifestyle, so he should be able to work it out. The thought sounded hollow in his head. Who was he kidding? He loved Elise, he had done ever since he was old enough to understand what it meant to care for another person…

perhaps even before that. As kids they'd always had a special bond. He'd looked after her when her parents worked late, watching while she practised her dance routines in the lounge room of the Johnson home but always being careful that Rich didn't catch him.

Rich. That was another great big mess he'd made. They'd been best friends since they were in kindergarten and now Rich didn't trust him at all. He should have come clean about his feelings for Elise, sought his blessing like a grown-up instead of sleeping with her behind his back. Now he'd lost them both; he'd lost his whole surrogate family.

Col's black suit hung over the chair at the dining table and with it a clean black shirt and black tie. He'd swelter in the summer heat, but there was a strong traditionalist streak in him that wouldn't accept anything but all black to be worn to a funeral…even if he would not be mourning the death of the person being buried. *What a mess.*

'Morning.' Elise shuffled from the bedroom, her hair sticking out in all directions like some weird imitation of a lion's mane.

She was wearing one of his T-shirts and it swam on her, obscuring her lovely figure with the exception of her lean dancer's legs. A lump lodged in his throat. He wanted to confess everything to her, his feelings, the desires he had about being with her…but there was no point. Even as he'd held her in his arms last night he knew it had to end. He had to be cruel to be kind. Theirs was a cord that needed to be cut and he had to be strong enough to do it.

'I need to head home,' she said, leaning against the side of the couch opposite him.

Figured—she was going to make it easy for him after all. He should have been relieved but her words scythed through him with an intensity that stole his breath. 'Fine.'

'I can't exactly go to a funeral in a T-shirt, now, can I?' She smiled softly.

He did a double take. 'What?'

'Your dad's funeral.' She tilted her head, brows furrowed. 'I thought it was today.'

'It is, but I didn't think you were coming.'

'I wouldn't be a very good friend if I left you to go on your own, now, would I?'

Friend. He almost let out the bitter laugh that rang in his head. Of course she wanted to comfort him as a friend…nothing more.

'I don't want you to come to the funeral.'

'Why not?' She planted her hands on her hips.

'He doesn't deserve to have you there, Ellie.' Col stood up and walked to the dining table where his outfit was laid out.

'I'm not going for him. I'm going for you.'

Col pulled on his shirt, taking his time to do the buttons up. He stepped into the trousers of the suit and immediately felt restricted. He hated wearing a suit and tie; it made him feel chained, controlled. But he was unlikely to feel comfortable at any part of today anyway. The suit was going to be the least of his discomfort.

'I said I'm going for you, Col.' She said his name emphatically. 'I care about you.'

He paused and looked at her, searching her face for any sign that she might be about to open up. She looked as though she was about to say something but her mouth snapped shut.

'How do you care about me? Do you care about me like a brother, a friend…?'

Her breath hitched but she said nothing. It was déjà vu all over again: he was asking her to clarify how she felt about him and she was staying silent. Did she feel anything at all for him beyond what she felt for her family? Or was he just a close friend who she happened to have slept with?

'*How?* I need to know.'

'Why are you doing this, Col?' She shook her head, turning away from him. 'You know I'm not good at this.'

'Because I deserve to know.' He swallowed and the words spilled forth as if something inside had broken and everything he'd ever felt was suddenly accessible and free flowing. 'I love you, Ellie, and I can't take not knowing if you love me back.'

She turned to him, face pale, and for the first time he'd seen her beautiful features twisted into anguish. He'd seen behind her mask; he'd pushed her until she'd shown him something real. In a second her face was stoic again, her lips pressed together as she gathered herself.

'I love you as a friend, Col. That's all I can give and I don't want to promise you more.'

He reached for his tie and slipped it around his neck, tightening it like a noose. At least now he knew, he could move on with his life and put the Johnson family behind him for good.

'It's best if you leave now.'

'Col—'

'I'll call downstairs and order you a taxi.'

He continued dressing himself, bending down to pull

on his dress socks and a pair of expensive leather dress
shoes he hardly ever wore. She stood there for a moment, rooted to the ground as if in silent protest. But,
as usual, no words came. The loss of her burned before she'd even vacated his hotel room. Looked as if
he would be grieving today after all.

He stood, adjusting the cuffs of his shirt while watching her from the corner of his eye. Was it his imagina-
tion or did a tear pool in her eye. No, impossible. Elise
Johnson didn't do tears.

By the time the taxi dropped Elise off she was fuming.
After the initial shock of finding out that Col loved her
had worn off, she was downright miffed. He'd known
what her upbringing was like—he'd been there for half
of it! Didn't he know that throwing your emotions out
there for the world to see was dangerous? Wasn't that
the very reason he'd been so poorly treated by his father…because the man hadn't been able to control his
emotions?

Stomping up to the front door, she cursed under her
breath. What was he thinking coming out and telling
her that he loved her? She flung the front door open and
let out a frustrated huff.

'Ellie?'

Her mother's voice wafted through the house along
with the scent of something baking in the oven. The
scent hit her with force; she knew it from a very long
time ago. Anzac cookies—her mother was baking the
oaty, golden syrupy treats of her childhood.

'Mum? What's going on?'

She came through to the kitchen to find her mother
standing at the sink wearing her pink and white striped

apron. Her hair was pulled into a ponytail; her eyes looked clearer than their usual bloodshot state. Was that humming she could hear?

'I know we usually go out for our weekly morning tea but I had a sudden urge to bake.' Her mother's voice was soft, hopeful.

'That's great. I always loved your Anzac cookies.' She dropped her bag onto the breakfast bar and hovered at the edge of the kitchen.

'Tea?' Her mother held up the kettle and Elise nodded.

'What's brought all this on?' Something had definitely shifted. It had been years since her mother had baked. It seemed like eons since she'd smiled.

Darlene drew a deep breath. 'I've started seeing someone.'

A rock hardened in the pit of Elise's stomach. How was it possible her mother had started seeing someone when she never left the house? Had she met some creep online? Myriad scenarios swirled in her mind.

'Not like *that*,' Darlene said. 'I've started seeing a psychologist, someone who specialises in treating members of the police force…ex-members in my case.'

'But I thought you hated talking about what happened to Dad.'

Her mother had not only shunned the court-appointed psychologist after her Internal Affairs hearing, but she'd avoided every offer of help from the police chief, her colleagues, family and friends. Eventually the offers dried up and she even managed to drive her own son away. Elise had stuck by her, but they had not once discussed the events that led to her father's death.

'It's uncomfortable for me, yes.' Darlene nodded.

'But I'm sick of feeling like this. Every day is a struggle and I think after five years it's about time I got back on my feet.'

Elise swallowed, a strange sensation ebbing through her. This was the most productive thing her mother had ever said. Hope blossomed in Elise's chest. Maybe she could be saved.

'How many sessions have you had?'

'Only four, but I'm going every week.'

'Why didn't you tell me?'

The oven timer beeped and Darlene went to the oven, pulling out the tray of golden cookies and placing them on a cutting board. She untied the back of her apron and hung it on the hook next to the stove. Elise watched her slow, precise movements.

'Why, Mum?'

Darlene came over to her and enveloped her in a hug. Her bony arms wrapped around Elise with the urgency of someone who hadn't been held in a long time. After a moment of stunned immobility, Elise hugged her back. When *was* the last time they hugged?

'I was worried I wouldn't do well and I didn't want to fail you again. This isn't the first time I've tried.'

'Really?' Elise pulled back, surprised.

'I tried about a year after...' She trailed off. 'Then again about twelve months ago. But I quit after two sessions. I was worried this time would be the same.'

'And?'

'I hope it's going to be different this time. I still have down days, but the sessions give me some relief.' Darlene stroked her daughter's hair. 'I know your father and I weren't very demonstrative while you and Rich were growing up but we loved you both very much. We wanted you to be strong and independent… I guess we thought that by being so tough on you it would make you that way.'

Tears pricked in Elise's eyes and out of instinct she blinked furiously to make them go away. It was the closest she'd come to crying in…she couldn't even remember how long.

'I regret not being more open with you and Rich,' Darlene continued. 'But it's not too late to start, is it?'

'No, it's not too late.' Elise looked into the grey eyes that were identical to her own. 'I'm so glad you're getting help.'

'Me too, baby. It's taken me a long time but I've realised that sometimes we need another person to help us change for the better.'

Elise's mind flickered to Col and his stubborn way of prodding her with questions. She'd resented him this morning, asking her to open up, to put herself way out of her comfort zone. He'd always done that, always challenged her, teased her, fought for her. She frowned.

'What's wrong? Have I upset you?' Darlene's concern brought her back to the present.

'It's nothing.' She plastered a bright smile on her face before she realised the irony of the situation. Here her mother was, after all the years, opening up and putting herself out there while Elise acted the same way she always did. 'Actually, there is something.'

Darlene released her, put a few cookies on a plate and brought it with the teapot to the kitchen table, where fresh irises sat in a fluted vase. Her mother must have brought them with her. Elise grabbed two teacups from the cupboard.

'Tell me.'

'Col is back in Australia at the moment.'

Darlene nodded. 'Yes, I know that.'

Elise's eyebrows shot up. 'How?'

'I got a call from your brother last night.'

Ah. Elise poured the tea and waited for her mother to continue.

'I gave him a good talking-to. He had no right to interfere with you and Col. That boy was always infatuated by you, you know.'

'Really?'

'Rich came to me when we took him in, said he was worried about Col being around you. But I trusted him. His father might have been a drunk but I know a good soul when I see one. Couldn't have been a police officer for so long without being able to pick the bad eggs from the good.' She smiled. 'He cared about you very much, always stuck up for you when you and your brother fought.'

'He did, didn't he?' For once a happy memory came to her, not the one of Col with bruises but the times that he'd stepped between her and Rich when an argument sprouted. He was always her protector.

'And he always used to take you to your ballet lessons. He claimed it was because he wanted to pitch in, but I knew it was more than that.' She sipped her tea. 'Why is he here?'

'Arthur's funeral is today.'

'And you're not going?' The old Darlene was back for a moment, all narrowed brows and pursed lips.

'I wanted to go but he said Arthur didn't deserve to have me there.' She swallowed. 'And I think I upset him.'

'How?'

'He told me he loved me.' She swiped a cookie, eager for something to distract her from the foreign feelings swirling. Her voice sounded strange, high pitched and unnatural. Perhaps this was what it sounded like to open up to someone.

'And...'

'And I told him I couldn't give him what he wanted.'

'Do you love him?'

The question rendered her mute. Self-protection was her instinct, her go-to move. But the ache in her chest was building; the pressure from holding her feelings in a tight, unreachable bundle was getting too much to bear.

'Love is not as confusing as people make it out to be.' Darlene gave a small smile.

Elise let out a shaky breath and traced the floral pattern of her china teacup with her finger. 'It's scary.'

'If it's scary then it means you care about him.'

'I do.' Her voice was barely above a whisper.

Was it possible that she'd loved Col all along and never allowed herself to see it? She remembered when he first walked into her studio a week ago. She'd wanted to scream at him for leaving her; she'd been appalled at how he could turn up without warning. But there had also been a tiny bubble in her chest, a delicate construct of hope and relief that had threatened to burst at the slightest provocation.

Except he hadn't burst it. He'd drawn her to him over and over, showing her that she could be intimate, showing her that she could help others, that she could talk about the past. No one else had ever been able to get so close, nor had anyone else continued to try after her constant rejection. He matched her in stubbornness and strength of will, but he also knew when to push her, when to hold her, when to comfort her.

'You know the answer to whether or not you love him, Ellie.' Darlene reached out and grabbed her daughter's hand, squeezing it tight. 'I want you to be happy. You deserve it—you've earned it for all you've done for our family.'

'I love you, Mum.' Her voice shook. She couldn't remember the last time she'd told anyone that she loved them—even her mother.

'I love you too.'

After Darlene left, Elise sat at the kitchen table as if she didn't have the strength left to move. She wasn't sure how long she'd been sitting there, but when she looked up the sun was starting to dip.

Only then did the enormity of her situation hit her. Col would be leaving for good. He was flying out tomorrow and she'd hurt him good enough that he was unlikely to come back for seconds...or thirds as the case might be. Hell, if his father hadn't died he might not have come back *this* time.

Her stomach churned. Never again would she wake up to his blue eyes, never again would she lose herself in his kiss, under the deft touch of his hands. But it was best for them both.

She loved him. When it'd happened she couldn't exactly pinpoint, but that strange churning sensation in her stomach that occurred whenever he was near finally had a name. She loved him and she'd let him go because she couldn't bear the thought of him waking up one morning in the future only to realise how broken she was.

It might happen after a fight, where he expected to talk about it. It could happen after a loss, where she'd be expected to show her sadness or vulnerability. What if they one day had a child and she was incapable of showing the love needed to nurture a young soul into life?

Her inadequacy was insurmountable; it filled her up and swallowed her feelings, hardening her to stone. He didn't deserve to end up with someone like her; he deserved better—someone who could love with all the unbridled passion and fury of a normal person.

Her eyes prickled and she ground her fists into them, surprised when they came away slicked with moisture. A fat tear fell onto her cheek and another followed, creating a path down to her jaw.

She rushed to the bathroom, shocked to see her face with eyes red-rimmed and cheeks glistening. She hadn't even cried at her father's funeral. She'd not shed a single tear, but now it was as if every tear she'd ever saved up was ready to be used. They spilled forth, unstoppable.

Her chest heaved with each sob, grief squeezing, pressing, aching within her. Suddenly the laughter came. It bubbled up until the tinkling sound filled the air. She was actually crying, something she had tried to do for so many years just to see if she could. But no matter how many times she watched *The Notebook*, *Beaches* or *Steel Magnolias* she could never even well up, let alone create a tear.

But the thought of letting Col go was enough to finally push her to the edge. In the past week he'd pushed her more than any other person, definitely more than the men she dated who were quick to label her faults and file her under 'too much effort'. And he'd certainly pushed her more than her parents.

Could she really give up the chance that maybe he could help her experience the full gamut of emotion?

He'd be arriving at the hotel soon and she had until tomorrow morning to convince him she'd been wrong. Scrap that—she had all night to *show* him.

CHAPTER TWELVE

AFTER THE FUNERAL Col stood in the dimming sunlight. The air was still heavy as a blanket over him. He sweltered in his suit, but he refused to loosen his tie. His father's girlfriend and a handful of scruffy-looking men in their fifties had been the only guests present. There were less than ten people total who'd shown up to mourn the life of Arthur Hill. *Less than ten too many.*

The already lean crowd thinned until it was just Col and the man who'd conducted the simple, non-religious service. They didn't speak, but instead stood next to one another lost in their own thoughts.

'Excuse me?'

A voice captured his attention and he turned to see the journalist from the conference with her camera man approaching. What the hell were they doing here?

'I'm Marina Shepard and I was wondering if I can ask you a few questions?' Her question posed as a statement, an introduction to the questions she was about to ask without waiting for permission.

'I don't do interviews,' Col said sharply. 'Particularly not at funerals.'

The journalist ignored him and stuck her recorder in Col's face. 'Is it true that you're the son of Arthur Hill?'

'No comment.'

'I understand Arthur was convicted of insurance fraud several years ago. How do you think that information would affect your shareholders?'

'I said, *no comment.*' His voice was a low, threatening growl.

He forced himself to stare straight ahead, fearing what he might do if he were to make eye contact with her.

'There's no need to be hostile,' she said, her tone indicating she enjoyed this part of her job very much. 'The people deserve to know the truth.'

'About a man who may or may not be related to some unknown person who died? How on earth is that something the people need to know?'

'I think you need to leave.' The man who'd conducted his father's service stepped in between them. 'This is very inappropriate.'

'I'm sure the shareholders of Hillam Technologies would like to understand the foundations on which the company was built. Arthur Hill was convicted of many crimes, as I'm sure you are aware, and one of those was insurance fraud. Don't you think the shareholders deserve to know that?'

Col turned and walked towards his car, his long legs crossing the plush green grass easily. But she would not be deterred.

'Mr Hillam!' The journalist was on his heels. 'Isn't that why you changed your name so no one would know the connection?'

Col stopped, took a breath and whirled around. 'I *am* Arthur Hill's son, but I became emancipated the second I could. Therefore, I was not legally tied to him at the time of the fraud nor at the time I started my company. None of the investigations at the time connected me or my business to him in any way. I do not support illegal activity. Now, I'll ask that you please leave me alone. I have no further comments.'

The wind seemed to run out of the journalist's sails; it was clearly not the emotional reaction she was hoping for.

Col stalked to his car and left the cemetery in a hurry. He drove through the city like a man possessed, the desire to flee growing stronger by the minute. He had to get out. Out of Australia, out of the mess he'd created with Elise, out of his own head. He left his car in the valet area of the hotel and went straight to his room to shower, change and pack.

The methodical actions of packing a suitcase calmed some of the prickling, nervous energy that flowed through him. But the need to escape was all consuming.

He'd continued to push Elise when he knew that she didn't have more to give, when she'd been nothing but transparent about the level of her feelings towards him. Why couldn't he accept that she didn't love him the way he loved her?

He took a deep breath and continued to fold and stack his clothing in the open suitcase on his hotel bed. He would be home soon and then he could put this trip far behind him. He'd throw himself into his work, leveraging the success of his talk at the conference to find new investors and to build the next big thing. Maybe he'd even head over to Singapore or Hong Kong for a bit.

His work would save him, as it always had. He'd stay in his office till late each night, working himself hard enough to guarantee an exhausted slumber. The weekends were tough, but he was rich and that would allow him to easily find company on the odd occasions that he wanted it. Plus he had Pete, his one true friend.

Col tried not to dwell on what a pathetic existence he led, one devoid of feeling and emotion. But he would not put himself in the path of rejection any more. Too many people had made it clear he couldn't be loved… that he wasn't quite good enough no matter how hard he tried. He didn't need to be told again.

A knock at his hotel-room door stopped the downward spiral of his thoughts. He was getting out of here, and that was that. He rolled the suitcase to the living area and opened the door.

'Would you like a turndown service, sir?' the young girl in the hotel uniform asked with a smile.

'I'll be checking out now,' Col replied, mustering a smile and walking past her to the elevator.

The reception desk processed his checkout quickly and offered to call the airport to see about changing his flight to LA to an earlier departure.

'Why don't you grab a drink in the bar and I'll send someone over with your new flight details? Would you like us to book you a driver as well?' The elegant woman behind the desk gestured to the cosy champagne bar on the other side of their huge reception area.

'Thank you. I have a rental car that needs to go back to the airport anyway. I'll drive myself.'

The last thing he wanted was to have nothing to do with his hands for the forty-five-plus minutes it would take to get from Southbank to Tullamarine at this time of evening. He left his suitcase with the staff and wandered over to the bar. It was the epitome of luxury hotel bars, somehow quiet despite being adjacent to the reception area and tastefully decorated in muted shades of gold, cream and chocolate.

Col ordered a gin and tonic and took a seat in the back, away from the young girls at the bar wearing too flashy dresses and OTT make-up who eyed him as he walked past. No other girl would even enter his mind until he'd got enough distance from Elise Johnson... like a minimum of two oceans' distance.

'Your gin and tonic, sir.' The waiter placed the heavy crystal glass down in front of him and Col raised it immediately to his lips.

Just one drink. Never more than one when he was feeling frustrated. The cold liquid slid down his throat, relaxing him. He let out a long breath and loosened his shoulders before pulling out an envelope from his jacket pocket.

He'd found an old photo of his mother at his father's house when he was cleaning out the closet. Col had only had the rarest of opportunities growing up to know what his mother looked like; his father had burned a lot of their old pictures in a drunken rage one night when Col had asked too many questions. His mother was a mystery to him, but here she stood with her long dark hair and light blue eyes the same as his. She was smiling. She looked...happy.

He traced the picture with his fingertip, strangely calmed by the image of her. She looked exactly as he'd imagined: warm and loving, smiling always. If only she hadn't died giving birth to him, how different his life could have been.

He wondered for a moment what it might have been

like to have been loved as a child. The sad thing was he couldn't even picture it. Col reached for his glass and took a sip. What would his life have looked like if his mother had lived?

Tension curled his hands into fists and he drew a deep breath to slow the thudding of his heart. All his life he'd shied away from situations where he could be rejected because of the way he was raised...except when it came to Elise. There was something deep within him that wouldn't let up when it came to her, something that wouldn't stop pushing him out of his comfort zone.

He swallowed. They both bore the scars of their parents' actions, and though he would have given anything to have Elise's life growing up he knew that it was far from perfect.

Yet she'd helped him to get out on that stage and do something that he knew he couldn't have done without her. She did care for him, that was obvious...but could she care for him in the way he wanted? Not as a friend, not even as a lover but as someone to whom she was wholly committed. He'd had enough of the 'sex only' arrangement; he wanted more and he wouldn't accept anything less.

But could he put himself out there one more time? Could he face her rejection again?

The bar around him grew louder as he pondered his thoughts. He could see the woman who'd helped him at Concierge approaching him. It was too late; he'd be leaving soon. Perhaps it was for the best.

He was about to get out of his chair and greet the woman as a flash of movement caught his attention. A blonde woman was jogging through the foyer, make-up streaked all over her face.

Ellie?

Elise jogged through the underground car park to the entertainment complex where Col's hotel was located. Her sneakers slapped against the concrete floor and she was turning heads as she sped by...but not in a good way. It seemed that once the crying had started it was quite difficult to make it stop. And since she'd never re-quired waterproof mascara before she now had panda-like black smudges around her eyes.

Appearance was a thing she never cared about a great deal; so long as her body was in good shape for her dancing she hadn't bothered with vanity. But now she was feeling self-conscious. Not because her make-up was smudged, not because she looked like a crazy madwoman, but because she was wearing her feelings for the whole world to see.

It would be worth it. When she showed Col how much she'd changed, this strange, fearful energy buzz-ing inside her would be worth it.

She tapped her foot impatiently as she waited for the elevator to take her out of the car park. Each moment felt as if it increased the risk of him slipping away. That, or the risk of losing her nerve.

The doors of the elevator pinged and she stepped into the hotel's foyer. There were people everywhere, suitcases dragging alongside the sound of heels click-ing against the marble floor. The air was filled with laughter, perfume and the excitement of a balmy sum-mer's eve.

Elise contemplated asking Reception to call ahead, but she figured it would be easier to surprise Col. Maybe he would have less opportunity to think about the way she'd treated him. If only she could get someone to buzz her up to the right level.

She jogged to the hotel elevators and looked around. A lady in a hotel uniform was waiting by the far end.

'Excuse me,' Elise said as she rushed over. 'I've left my key in my room. I need to get up to level—'

'You'll need to go to the concierge desk, miss. Even if I get you to the right floor, you won't get in your room without a key. You need to—

'My husband's in the room. I just need to get up to the right floor.'

'You'll need to go to the concierge desk.' The older woman looked her up and down. 'They can issue a replacement key.'

'Please.' Elise wrung her hands. 'I don't want people to see me like this.'

Her voice was steady out of years of practice, but the woman's face softened. 'Just this once. Next time you use the concierge desk, okay?'

'Okay.' She nodded. 'Thank you so much.'

The elevator opened and they stepped in. The woman swiped her access card and Elise pushed the button for the top floor. As they sped up the floor numbers ticked over quickly and she held her breath.

The penthouse floor was quiet; the silence almost made Elise turn back. Silence meant thinking, and at this point that was not a very good idea. She made it to Col's door and knocked. Silence.

'Col, it's me. I'm sorry.' She knocked again.

The door flew open and Elise was met with the wary face of a hotel staffer. 'Is this your room?'

'No, I ugh…' She looked into the room and saw the pile of sheets and towels on the floor. 'I'm looking for the man who was staying in this room.'

'He's checked out.' She smiled in apology.

'When?'

She shrugged and looked at her watch. 'Twenty minutes ago…maybe half an hour.'

He'd be halfway to the airport by now. How would she be able to catch him? She turned, looking down the long corridor with its stylish gold trimmings and gentle light. It created a fantasy, one where people's lives were elegant and perfect and kept together.

A hard ball knotted in her stomach. She'd stuffed things up with Col on so many occasions that there would be no way he'd accept her apology. Why should he? Regret filtered through her, pulling on her limbs until it felt hard to take each step. She walked slowly back to the elevator.

What would she do now? She pushed the call button and leant her back against the wall between two elevators. How could she go back to her former life when she'd finally started to understand what it meant to feel something deep and terrifying and real for another person? She would never find that again. Col was the only man who'd been able to tap into that side of her. The elevator pinged and she turned as the doors slid open.

'Going down?' A deep, male voice caught her attention.

Elise looked up, eyes blurred with tears. 'I thought you'd checked out.'

'I have.' Col stepped back to let her into the elevator.

The doors slid closed behind her. 'Then why are you here?'

'I saw you in the lobby—at least I thought it was you.' He sighed. 'I saw a blonde woman running like the devil himself was chasing her, and she had black make-up all over her face. Somehow I knew it was you under all that muck.'

'You did?' Her voice wavered, the hope she'd tried her whole life to supress simmering close to the surface. Too close.

'What did you want to talk about?'

She pressed her palm against the elevator emergency stop button and the cabin slowed to a halt. 'I've been doing some thinking and I wanted to share something with you.'

'You better hope that button doesn't set off any alarms.' He sounded aloof, but the curiosity in his eyes was unmistakable.

'There was something that I never told you about Dad's death, something that I think you deserve to know. I'm not going to hold anything back from you anymore. I hope this proves it to you.'

'I thought your dad's death was a freak accident?'

She fiddled with the lengths of her ponytail, fighting the urge to shut down. 'He and Mum were on a raid together. It was a drug bust, a fairly big one from what I remember. They'd been tracking this particular group for a while and Mum came across some information about where they were hiding some of their product. She was in charge of the operation and Dad was going as backup.

'They thought they cleared the place and Mum ordered Dad and another cop to search the backyard. But they'd missed someone. There was a man hiding out in the backyard and he had a gun. He killed Dad and wounded the other policeman. Mum always blamed herself. She was cleared by the Internal Affairs hearing but she never went back to work.'

'Why didn't you tell me any of this? I thought it was a weapon malfunction—that's what Rich told me.'

'That's what we were telling everyone. Mum couldn't bear the truth and the force didn't want those kinds of details getting out to the media. They kept it quiet because Mum and Dad were both respected members since they graduated high school.' She bit down on her lip. 'We were never allowed to talk about it, to ask questions. Mum refused to see a psychologist and she got worse and worse until Rich left because he couldn't take it anymore. She developed a gambling problem…that's why the ballet school was in a bad state. She gambled away all our savings, everything I'd stashed away and almost all of Dad's payout.'

'How could you not have told me this? After all your mother did for me…why didn't you tell me?'

'She didn't want us to tell anyone. After I quit ballet Rich left for England. I had to suck it up and keep everyone going. The studio was my outlet in the beginning, but I was young and stupid. I thought it would be better to have a mortgage on the studio and keep some money in our accounts in case anything happened… I had no idea she'd blow the whole lot.'

'My God, Ellie. I was sitting on the other side of the world completely oblivious.' He talked as if to himself. 'I have more money than I know what to do with. I should have helped you sooner.'

'I thought you were paying for my services.' She

squeezed her eyes shut for a moment. 'You told me it wasn't charity.'

'It wasn't charity.' He paused. 'I knew having you close by would calm me enough to make the presentation.'

'I never felt like I was a calming presence. You've been anything but calm since you got to Australia.'

'That's because I'm chasing the impossible.'

Elise rested her hand on his wrist but didn't say anything. Her heart was hammering as if fighting death itself, her blood roared and her stomach tilted. It was as if every atom of her being resisted opening up to him, resisted facing the truth.

'Why do you find it so hard to come to me for help?' he asked.

'No beating around the bush, hey?' She took a deep breath. 'I'm not very good at asking *anyone* for help, Col. It's not just you—don't take it personally.'

'I want to take it personally.' He shook off her hand and rubbed the back of his neck.

'Why would you want that?'

'I want you to lump everyone else together and treat *me* differently. I want you to at least tell me what's going on.'

'It's not that easy.'

'Yes, it is. You pick up the phone and you call me. Sounds pretty damn simple to me.' He touched her face, swiping a thumb over her cheek. Her lip trembled and her breath hitched.

'I love you,' she blurted out, before clamping her hand over her mouth.

'Yes, we've established this.' He withdrew his hand. 'You love me as a friend.'

'That's true.' She nodded. 'But I also love you as something else.'

Col's eyes flashed but he kept his distance. She could see the torment in his face and it made her chest ache to think she had caused him to feel like that...not just now but over and over. Should she really be telling him how she felt?

'Spit it out.' His voice was quiet but it made her draw her shoulders back and look him in the eye.

'I love you like everything. Like a best friend, like a lover, like life support.' She resisted the urge to close her eyes and put her hands over her face. Her mask had no place here. 'I love you like I've never loved anyone else.'

'Then why have you been denying it?'

She bit down on her lip, trying to think of why she'd been keeping it locked away as though it were her life's greatest secret.

He sighed. 'I'm supposed to be leaving to catch a plane.'

'Then why did you come after me?'

'Because I'm an idiot. I can't keep myself away from you.' He sighed bitterly. 'I can't learn that lesson.'

She took a deep breath. 'You know what my house was like growing up. Mum and Dad weren't very de-monstrative.'

'I know.' He nodded. 'But that doesn't change what *I* need.'

'Nor should it. But I'm telling you that's why I was denying it...because I didn't know how to deal with all these crazy, illogical feelings. I thought it was wrong to be vulnerable, Mum always brought me up to be strong, to be a rock.'

'You *are* a rock, Ellie.' His face softened. 'But I don't

want to be with a rock. I want to be with that girl who completely lost herself in that hotel room upstairs. I want to know that if we have a fight you'll be able to talk to me about it afterwards. I want to know if you have a crappy day that you won't hide it from me. I want to know you won't stop letting me in.'

'I won't.' She grabbed his hand.

'I don't want to wake up one day and realise I don't know anything you're thinking.'

'I promise, I will work at it every day.' Her eyes welled but she beamed up at him. 'Look what you've done to me—you made me cry!'

'You're the only woman I know who would sound so excited about having a man make her cry.' He smiled, lacing his fingers in hers.

'I *am* excited. I thought I was doing the right thing by letting you go back to the States. I was worried that I wouldn't be able to live up to what you need.'

'And what do you need, Ellie? It's not all about me.'

'A push. I know I'm not perfect, but I'm going to try. I need you to keep pushing me.'

Her mind switched to thoughts more illicit and heat bloomed in her cheeks.

'Anything else?' He cocked a brow, clearly noticing her change of thought.

'Multiple orgasms?'

A smile tugged at the corners of his lips and he ran a hand along his stubbled jaw. 'I thought they affected your judgement.'

'I want to be affected.' She blinked the moisture from her eyes. 'I want to be vulnerable and passionate and all those things I've been afraid of up until now.'

He stood, scooping her up in his arms. His lips

crushed down to hers with burning intensity, he opened her up, took from her the passion he deserved and that she wanted to give for the rest of her life. He pressed her back against the elevator wall.

'Are you going to miss your plane?' she asked, pressing her face against his neck.

He shrugged. 'There will be another one.'

'How are we going to make it work? I can't leave Mum here by herself.'

He pressed his lips to her temple. 'I love you, Ellie. That's how it will work.'

She wrapped her arms around his neck and pulled his face close to hers. 'I love you too.'

'Besides, I can afford my own plane.' He laughed. 'And I'll move my whole goddamn company here if that's what it takes.'

'You can do that?' Warmth spread through her, loosening her limbs so that she melted against him. For the first time in her life she felt exposed and protected at the same time. She knew deep down in her heart she would do everything in her power to make Col feel loved and that he would unravel her insecurities bit by bit.

'I can do anything now.' He pressed his hand against her lower back, drawing her to him. 'Now let's find somewhere we can get started on those orgasms.'

EPILOGUE

FOR SOMEONE WHO'D spent the past week relocating his office from one continent to another, Col was surprisingly energised. In record time he'd sourced a new location in Melbourne's central business district for his company headquarters, set up a satellite office in New York to make sure all of his workers still had a job *and* moved his personal effects from his apartment to Elise's unit. They would look for a new place, of course, but there were other more important matters to attend to first.

He patted the bulging pocket of his dress trousers where a small, velvet box was hidden. His palms were slick but he'd never felt so sure about anything in his whole life. Tonight he was going to propose to Elise Johnson, and there was not a shred of doubt in his mind how she would feel about it. He bit back a grin.

'I wish Jasmine and Grant would arrive so we can order,' Elise said, fiddling with her cutlery. 'I missed lunch today and I'm *starving*.'

'She texted me before. It sounds like her rehearsals ran overtime.' Missy sat across from Col and Elise, her red hair gleaming in the restaurant's cosy lighting.

As if on cue Jasmine rushed into the restaurant,

cheeks pink and hair in a slick ballerina bun. Her fiancé, Grant Farley, was close behind.

'I'm so sorry we're late,' Jasmine said. 'The director's working us to the bone.'

'Only one week till opening night,' Grant added, slipping Jasmine's coat from her shoulders and slinging it over the back of her chair.

The pair settled down and the three girls immediately started talking about the ballet studio's upcoming cabaret night. Col watched Elise, enamoured with the way her grey eyes sparkled when she talked about her studio, which, thanks to a little financial planning, was starting to thrive again.

'They're always talking shop, these girls.' Grant chuckled. 'Such workaholics.'

The conversation dimmed as a waiter arrived at their table to deliver a bottle of champagne and take everyone's orders. Col grabbed the bottle from the ice bucket and eased the cork out with a satisfying pop. The girls immediately held their flutes out for the sparkling liquid.

'Yes, please!' Elise said with a bright smile on her face.

'Don't skimp either,' replied Missy. 'It's been a *long* day.'

Once the bubbles were distributed Col took a deep breath and stood up. 'I'd like to make a toast.'

Elise looked at him curiously. Toasts were not his thing, in fact this would be the first toast he'd ever made, but a lot had changed since he'd taken the stage at the technology conference three months ago. Public speaking still made him nervous, but if he were to feel

comfortable declaring anything in public, his love for
Elise would be it.

The table waited for him to speak, champagne flutes
at the ready.

'Elise and I organised this dinner to celebrate the
move of my company to Melbourne *and* to say thank
you for keeping the ballet studio going while she was
helping me in New York.' Col drew a slow breath. 'But
I have a different agenda for calling you here tonight.'

The table was so silent you could have heard a pin
drop and the ambient noise of the restaurant faded away
into nothingness. All Col could hear was the intake of
breath from Elise, who looked up at him with saucer-
like eyes.

'Not too long ago the idea of standing up to give a
toast in the middle of a restaurant would have made
me run a mile. However, if it weren't for that fear I
might never have been desperate enough to come to
Elise for help.'

'Gee, thanks, Col,' she said, rolling her eyes. The
table chuckled and Col winked at Elise.

'Elise has helped me a lot over the years,' Col continued, his tone suddenly serious. 'And I'd like to think
that more recently I've helped her as well.'

Elise nodded vigorously. 'You have.'

Col slipped the velvet box from his pocket and got
down on one knee. Her breath hitched as she looked
from Col to the box and back again. Inside, nestled
in plush satin, was a diamond solitaire surrounded by
small emeralds that trailed down the sides of the band.
He'd known the second he laid eyes on it that it was
perfect for her. Beautiful yet different.

'Elise, I want us to keep helping each other. I want us to help one another be the best versions of ourselves.'

Tears sparkled in her eyes. She was as still as a statue, her face alight with joy. He would propose to her again and again if only to be rewarded with that look.

'Will you marry me, Elise Johnson?'

A tear slid down her cheek. 'Yes.'

He stood and slipped the ring onto her finger, the thudding of his heart even louder than the cheers coming from their table and from the tables around them.

'You didn't have to do it in public,' she said, throwing her arms around his neck. 'I respect that you're a private person.'

'I know.' He brought his lips down to hers, breaking away to laugh when Grant let out a loud wolf whistle. 'But I wanted to make sure your judgement wasn't clouded.'

'Is that so?' A sly smile spread over her lips.

'And if we were home alone…' he bent his head to whisper in her ear '…nothing could possibly have stopped me pleasuring you until you didn't have a coherent thought left in your head.'

'Judgement is overrated.' She bit down on her lower lip, eyes glimmering. 'Put me down for an extra-large order of incoherence.'

'Anything for you, Ellie.'

* * * * *

Mills & Boon® Hardback

October 2014

ROMANCE

An Heiress for His Empire	Lucy Monroe
His for a Price	Caitlin Crews
Commanded by the Sheikh	Kate Hewitt
The Valquez Bride	Melanie Milburne
The Uncompromising Italian	Cathy Williams
Prince Hafiz's Only Vice	Susanna Carr
A Deal Before the Altar	Rachael Thomas
Rival's Challenge	Abby Green
The Party Starts at Midnight	Lucy King
Your Bed or Mine?	Joss Wood
Turning the Good Girl Bad	Avril Tremayne
Breaking the Bro Code	Stefanie London
The Billionaire in Disguise	Soraya Lane
The Unexpected Honeymoon	Barbara Wallace
A Princess by Christmas	Jennifer Faye
His Reluctant Cinderella	Jessica Gilmore
One More Night with Her Desert Prince...	Jennifer Taylor
From Fling to Forever	Avril Tremayne

MEDICAL

It Started with No Strings...	Kate Hardy
Flirting with Dr Off-Limits	Robin Gianna
Dare She Date Again?	Amy Ruttan
The Surgeon's Christmas Wish	Annie O'Neil

ROMANCE

Ravelli's Defiant Bride	Lynne Graham
When Da Silva Breaks the Rules	Abby Green
The Heartbreaker Prince	Kim Lawrence
The Man She Can't Forget	Maggie Cox
A Question of Honour	Kate Walker
What the Greek Can't Resist	Maya Blake
An Heir to Bind Them	Dani Collins
Becoming the Prince's Wife	Rebecca Winters
Nine Months to Change His Life	Marion Lennox
Taming Her Italian Boss	Fiona Harper
Summer with the Millionaire	Jessica Gilmore

HISTORICAL

Scars of Betrayal	Sophia James
Scandal's Virgin	Louise Allen
An Ideal Companion	Anne Ashley
Surrender to the Viking	Joanna Fulford
No Place for an Angel	Gail Whitiker

MEDICAL

200 Harley Street: Surgeon in a Tux	Carol Marinelli
200 Harley Street: Girl from the Red Carpet	Scarlet Wilson
Flirting with the Socialite Doc	Melanie Milburne
His Diamond Like No Other	Lucy Clark
The Last Temptation of Dr Dalton	Robin Gianna
Resisting Her Rebel Hero	Lucy Ryder

Mills & Boon® Hardback

November 2014

ROMANCE

A Virgin for His Prize	Lucy Monroe
The Valquez Seduction	Melanie Milburne
Protecting the Desert Princess	Carol Marinelli
One Night with Morelli	Kim Lawrence
To Defy a Sheikh	Maisey Yates
The Russian's Acquisition	Dani Collins
The True King of Dahaar	Tara Pammi
Rebel's Bargain	Annie West
The Million-Dollar Question	Kimberly Lang
Enemies with Benefits	Louisa George
Man vs. Socialite	Charlotte Phillips
Fired by Her Fling	Christy McKellen
The Twelve Dates of Christmas	Susan Meier
At the Chateau for Christmas	Rebecca Winters
A Very Special Holiday Gift	Barbara Hannay
A New Year Marriage Proposal	Kate Hardy
A Little Christmas Magic	Alison Roberts
Christmas with the Maverick Millionaire	Scarlet Wilson

MEDICAL

Playing the Playboy's Sweetheart	Carol Marinelli
Unwrapping Her Italian Doc	Carol Marinelli
A Doctor by Day...	Emily Forbes
Tamed by the Renegade	Emily Forbes

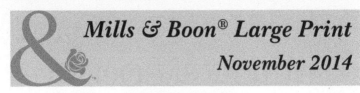

Mills & Boon® Large Print
November 2014

ROMANCE

Christakis's Rebellious Wife	Lynne Graham
At No Man's Command	Melanie Milburne
Carrying the Sheikh's Heir	Lynn Raye Harris
Bound by the Italian's Contract	Janette Kenny
Dante's Unexpected Legacy	Catherine George
A Deal with Demakis	Tara Pammi
The Ultimate Playboy	Maya Blake
Her Irresistible Protector	Michelle Douglas
The Maverick Millionaire	Alison Roberts
The Return of the Rebel	Jennifer Faye
The Tycoon and the Wedding Planner	Kandy Shepherd

HISTORICAL

A Lady of Notoriety	Diane Gaston
The Scarlet Gown	Sarah Mallory
Safe in the Earl's Arms	Liz Tyner
Betrayed, Betrothed and Bedded	Juliet Landon
Castle of the Wolf	Margaret Moore

MEDICAL

200 Harley Street: The Proud Italian	Alison Roberts
200 Harley Street: American Surgeon in London	Lynne Marshall
A Mother's Secret	Scarlet Wilson
Return of Dr Maguire	Judy Campbell
Saving His Little Miracle	Jennifer Taylor
Heatherdale's Shy Nurse	Abigail Gordon

MILLS & BOON®

Why shop at millsandboon.co.uk?

Each year, thousands of romance readers find their perfect read at millsandboon.co.uk. That's because we're passionate about bringing you the very best romantic fiction. Here are some of the advantages of shopping at www.millsandboon.co.uk:

* **Get new books first**—you'll be able to buy your favourite books one month before they hit the shops

* **Get exclusive discounts**—you'll also be able to buy our specially created monthly collections, with up to 50% off the RRP

* **Find your favourite authors**—latest news, interviews and new releases for all your favourite authors and series on our website, plus ideas for what to try next

* **Join in**—once you've bought your favourite books, don't forget to register with us to rate, review and join in the discussions

Visit **www.millsandboon.co.uk**
for all this and more today!